Ask Amy Green

SUMMER SECRETS

SARAH WEBB

D1411912

CANDLEWICK PRESS

To Judy Blume

for a life-changing lunch in 1996

and a lifelong friend in Margaret

Copyright © 2011 by Sarah Webb

First U.S. paperback edition 2012

Library of Congress Cataloging-in-Publication Data is available.

Library of Congress Catalog Card Number 2010039171

ISBN 978-0-7636-5071-1 (hardcover)
ISBN 978-0-7636-5705-5 (paperback)

12 13 14 15 16 17 BVG 10 9 8 7 6 5 4 3 2 1

Printed in Berryville, VA, U.S.A.

This book was typeset in ITC Giovanni.

Candlewick Press
99 Dover Street
Somerville, Massachusetts 02144

visit us at www.candlewick.com

Hi.

Welcome to *Summer Secrets*. A good chunk of this book is set in Miami; the rest is set in West Cork, Ireland — my favorite place in the whole world. My mum and dad have a house in Castletownshend, West Cork — a small fishing village with a shop and two pubs — and we've been going there on our holidays since I was five.

I love swimming in the (very nippy!) sea, sailing and exploring the coastline and islands in our wooden fishing boat, the *Amy-Rose* (named after my daughter). But most of all, I love sitting on the beautiful "Station" Beach and reading or just daydreaming.

I've tried to give a little taste of West Cork in this book. Haven House, where Amy and her family stay, doesn't actually exist, but Lough Ine (you pronounce it Lock Eye-n) is real, all right. It's a stunning tidal lake where you can go swimming or moonlight kayaking. I invented Lough Ine village, but there really is an island in the middle of the lake, and I've often gazed at it from the shore, wondering what it would be like to live there.

I hope you enjoy *Summer Secrets*. It is full of secrets and surprises, just like West Cork.

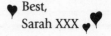 Best,
Sarah XXX

♥ Chapter 1

"It's *soooo* unfair," I moan, my head on Seth's lap. We're lying on Killiney Beach, our special place. Seth's my boyfriend (I love saying that — boyfriend!), and it was on this very beach that I first noticed his amazing sky-blue eyes, not to mention his washboard stomach. His dog, Billy, is rolling around in the sand beside us, yapping happily.

Seth winds my hair around his fingers. "I know, but it's only three weeks."

"*Only* three weeks? A lot can happen in three weeks."

We've only been together for nine weeks. So if you look at it that way, three weeks is a very long time — 33.3 (recurring) percent of our relationship, to be exact. Sorry, I like math. Geeky, I know, but a girl has to have her vices!

I'm off on holiday with my crazy family—all of them. And when your parentals are divorced, like mine, and both have new partners, that's a lot of people. Dave—my mum's boyfriend—has even invited his posh sister and her family along too.

The shared family holiday was Dad's idea. He claimed it would be a bonding experience for everyone after certain recent events—but it sounds like a nightmare to me. Luckily, Clover, my seventeen-year-old aunt, is coming along too. Otherwise I'd go completely crazy.

And get this: while I'm stuck in Cork for two weeks on the holiday from hell, Seth's off for three weeks to a big farmhouse just outside Rome. They're flying out this evening. His mum, Polly, is teaching photography at this arty-farty place that sounds like a weirdie commune to me—all hippy-dippy veggie food and workshops on connecting with your inner child. (Are they serious? Who'd want to do that?)

Seth is smiling down at me, his blond hair flopping over his eyes. There's a new smattering of cute sun freckles over the bridge of his nose. "I'll write to you," he says.

"E-mail, you mean."

"That too. But I meant pen and paper. Envelope, stamp, the works."

"Why would you do that? It's a lot of hassle. Do they even have post boxes in the wilds of Italia?"

He shrugs. "I like letters." The tops of his ears have flared a little and he looks away. "But e-mail is fine," he says quietly.

Poor Seth, he probably has his letters all planned out. He's a bit of a Boy Scout sometimes: likes to be prepared. Maybe he was thinking of sending me some sketches too. He's brilliant at art. And now I've gone and squashed his idea.

"No, you're right," I say. "Let's write proper letters."

"Cool." He stops for a moment before adding, "As long as you can read my handwriting." His mouth twists a little. "And I can't spell, either."

I've been wondering about this for a while. His texts are full of spelling mistakes. "Are you dyslexic?" I ask.

He shrugs. "I guess. I went to this psychologist, and I had to have extra reading and spelling classes in primary school, but Mum doesn't want to make a big deal of it. I wanted to drop out of Irish, but she wouldn't let me. You need it to work for RTÉ. She rang and asked them."

"RTÉ?" (Radio Telefís Éireann is Ireland's national telly and radio station.) "You want to be an actor?" I grab a piece of driftwood and start singing "Summer Nights" into it. The school drama club is doing *Grease* in September. Mills and I are determined to be in it, mainly 'cause it means: one, skipping a double Irish class on a Friday afternoon for rehearsals, and, two, meeting cute older boys. I have Seth, of course, but Mills is dying to meet someone, and she likes her boys "mature."

Seth would make a brilliant Danny if only I could persuade him to audition. He's not exactly Mr. School and barely goes to all his classes as it is. I can see him now, though, up on the stage, hair slicked back, leather jacket, tight black jeans, his slim hips wiggling — oh, baby!

"Earth calling Amy; come in, Amy." Seth is staring at me.

My eyes are resting on his hips, and I drag them away. How embarrassing! I cover my pink cheeks with my hands. "I think I've had a bit too much sun," I say. "Sorry, what were you saying about the telly?"

"Radio. I want to work in radio."

"As a DJ?"

"No. Behind the scenes. Production or research."

Just then my mobile beeps. I read the text message:

AMY, HOME NOW! U MUST PACK. R U STILL AT CLOVER'S? UR MOTHER!

"Oops," I say, climbing to my feet and brushing sand off my bum. I haven't even been to Clover's yet.

Seth puts his arms around my waist and tries to pull me back down onto the sand.

I shriek. "Unhand me, Casanova."

"It'll cost you." He grins up at me. "A kiss."

My tummy does a flip. Clover's comprehensive kissing lessons are certainly coming in useful. He loosens his grip on my waist. I put one leg on either side of his and sit on his lap; then, leaning forward, I tilt my head a little. Our lips connect. *Zing!* There goes the electricity again, radiating out from my lips; within seconds, my whole body feels tingly. I open my mouth a bit and feel the warm tip of his tongue against mine. Then —

Yap, yap, yap. Billy barks in my ear and jumps on my back.

I break away from Seth, startled. "Ow." I rub my skin through my T-shirt. He has sharp claws.

"Bad dog," Seth tells Billy, pulling him away from me by his collar. I give my mouth a quick wipe with the back of my hand.

When Billy has finally calmed down, Seth says,

"Sorry about that. I don't know what's wrong with him today."

My mobile starts to ring. It's Mum. Double oops.

"Angry parental alert. I really have to skedaddle. I'll text you the address of the holiday house. And the landline." I groan. "Two weeks of hell."

He shrugs. "It might be fun."

I pull a face. "Yeah, right. But at least Clover's going—that's something."

Seth grins. "She's a bad influence. Stay out of jail. And Amy?"

"Yes?"

"I'll miss you."

♥ Chapter 2

I make it over to Clover's just in time to "help" her pack by bouncing up and down on her acid-green suitcase to close it.

"Holy cow, you must be heavy, Beanie," she says, frowning at the case. "Your bum is denting it."

I jump off and it pings open, firing her clothes onto the floor, like guests jumping out at a surprise party.

"Beanie!" She scoops the T-shirts and tank tops into her tanned arms and dumps them back in the suitcase.

"Aren't you going to fold them, Clover? They'll get wrinkled."

"You sound just like your mum," she says, but she takes them back out and begins to fold them. I help her, ironing out the wrinkles with my hands, then folding each top into a neat square on the bed.

Clover smiles. "You could so get a job at Benetton."

Once we've packed the green case, Clover reaches underneath her bed and pulls out a slightly smaller one and a matching vanity case. I think it's what they call a suite of luggage. I wonder if they fit inside one another, like Russian dolls. That would be cute.

Dusting down the new suitcase with her hand, she sends dust mites spiraling into the air, like microscopic ballerinas. She wiggles her nose and sneezes.

"Bless you!" I say automatically.

She beams at me. "Aren't you sweet? Now, tip my knicker drawer into this smaller case, Bean Machine, and I'll pack my makeup."

I stare at her. "The whole drawer? We're only going for two weeks, Clover, not a year."

She shrugs. "A girl needs choice. My bikinis are in there too. And I'll need to pack my laptop and work stuff. That reminds me, Beanie: what do you know about Efa Valentine?"

"The film star?" Efa Valentine is a rising Hollywood star. She's Irish too and the same age as Clover. She was nominated for an Oscar last year. She didn't get it — she was up against Kate Winslet and Cate Blanchett — but it made her even more famous.

Clover nods. "I'm interviewing her in Cork city while we're on hols. The mag thought it was a good idea, as we're the same age. Want to tag along?"

I nod eagerly. Silly question.

"I'm a nervous wreck," she admits. "My very first interview and it has to be a big movie star like Efa Valentine. Saskia was supposed to be doing it, but Saffy's making her prepare for her big interview in Miami." Saffy is Clover's editor at the *Goss* magazine.

"Saskia?" I ask.

"New intern at the magazine." Clover puts on a posh marbles-in-the-mouth voice. "Saskia Davenport, darling." She wrinkles her nose. "Daddy owns half of Ireland." Then she adds, in her normal voice, "Six foot, red lips, jet-black hair, Cleopatra fringe: your average nightmare. Has some sort of big-deal journalism degree. She's already asked Saffy if she can *help* me with the agony aunt pages."

"What did Saffy say?"

"That I had it covered. But my days are numbered — Saskia's fiercely ambitious." Clover sounds a bit glum.

"Mills is off to Miami too," I say brightly, to change the subject. "Remember Marlon and Betty Costigan?"

Clover smiles. "*Remember?* I still have nightmares

about those kiddlywinks. Especially after the Louis Walsh episode."

"*X Factor* Louis?"

"Uh-huh. I must have told you about it."

I shake my head. "Nope."

"OK. Well, first of all, they both refused to go to bed. I tried bribing them with sweets, but that just made them even more hyper. Anyway, one of Louis Walsh's boy bands happened to come on the telly, and Marlon said that Louis was his godfather. I thought he was just trying to impress me, so I told him to stop being daft. And he said he'd prove it. He ran off and I forgot all about it. Then the next thing I knew: *ding-dong.* And there he was, Louis Walsh, standing on the doorstep, a big impish grin on his face. He was smaller than I expected, but much cuter."

"No! What did you do?"

"I invited him in, of course. Marlon got out his karaoke SingStar, and we all had a great laugh. Ria Costigan walked into the living room at midnight, and Betty was prancing around to "Mamma Mia" in her heels, still high as a kite from all those sweets. I think Ria had been drinking, 'cause she was swaying a bit. When she saw what was going on, she sobered up pretty quickly, though. She called me irresponsible and practically threw me out of the house! And that was the paddy last time I babysat for the Costigans."

I wince and then laugh. "Holy drama-rama! I'm not surprised they never had you back. No wonder they've gone for someone like Mills this time."

Clover looks intrigued. "Explain."

"She's babysitting for them this summer. In Miami, no less."

"Go on."

"Rex, Marlon and Betty's dad, is casting a new Matt Munroe film called *Life Swap*, which is set in Miami, and Ria's involved in the publicity for Matt's latest movie, *Just Add Water*. Mills might even get to meet him and—"

"Rewind. Did you say *Matt Munroe*?"

I nod.

"That's who Saskia's interviewing!" Clover says. "Matt Munroe from *West Dream High*."

I gasp. "Wow. Lucky thing. Cosmic heart-flutters. It's a pity you're not doing it, Clover. You could have hooked up with Mills while you were over there." Yikes, probably not the best thing to have said under the circumstances. Clover's face drops. "But Efa's cool too," I add quickly.

She sighs. "Cork's hardly Miami. But Saskia's got

a lot more experience — which reminds me, I need to practice my interview technique. Can I quiz you, Beanie?"

My mobile beeps. Oops. Mum again.

"Sure. But right now I have to run. We're leaving for Cork first thing."

"I'm driving down in the morning too, but it won't be as early. Need my beauty sleep. So I'll see you there, Beans. Hope you survive the journey."

I don't think she's joking.

♥ Chapter 3

"Seth says he'll miss me," I tell Mills that evening. I clutch my heart and flutter my eyelashes. "Swoon!"

Mills has popped round to say good-bye. She's off to Miami tomorrow night, so we won't see each other for ages. Mum nearly didn't let her into the house; she's gone mad with all the packing. You should see the place. There are half-packed bags in every single room. She's run out of proper zip-up ones, and now she's throwing things into anything she can find: grocery bags, canvas toy bags, my old Barbie schoolbag from when I was five — even nappy bags. You'd swear we were going on safari to darkest Africa or trekking across the Sahara or something.

When Mills rang the doorbell, Mum would only open the front door a crack, as if Mills were some sort of violent criminal.

"You can have ten minutes," she told her.

"Why don't I help Amy pack?" Mills offered eagerly. "I'm great at folding clothes."

Mum looked at her suspiciously. "OK."

Now every time Mum peers round the door, Mills carefully folds a T-shirt and hands it to me. We've been passing the same one backward and forward for fifteen minutes, and Mum hasn't copped on yet.

I'm only allowed to bring one bag of clothes — one! How Cruella De Vil is that? And my sports bag for all my books and music. I hope Mum doesn't spot the *Amy loves Seth* in the big love heart. Mills graffitied my bag on the last day of school.

"So did you get a good-bye kiss?" Mills asks, her eyes sparkling.

I open my mouth to say something, but she gets in first.

"What was it like? Was his tongue all hot and sticky?" Mills is so excited; she's hopping around like a little kid who needs the loo.

"Shush!" I tell her. "Otherwise Mum's going to kick you out." I grab a pair of shorts and fling them into the bag, followed by my new white jeans. I'm not all that keen on the jeans — they're a bit tight — but Clover made me buy them. She said they're a summer-wardrobe staple, like a little black dress in the winter. I'm not convinced.

Suddenly, Mum appears in the doorway. "How are you getting on, Amy?"

"Nearly finished."

"Good — you can help me with Evie's clothes when you're done." She disappears down the corridor.

"Better slow down," I say to Mills. "Or else she'll have me counting Onesies. Deadly boring."

Mills isn't going to be put off. "Tell me about the kiss. What was it like?"

"Nice."

"*Nice?* Amy!" She hits me with a silver belt.

"Ouch!" I stroke my arm. The buckle's left a red mark on my skin.

"Sorry."

"'S OK. But there's no need to get violent. We only kissed for a few seconds. Billy wasn't impressed."

"Billy?"

"Seth's dog, remember? I think he was jealous. We were just getting started and he jumped on top of me."

Mills's eyes widen. "Seth?"

"No, you sap; he's not some kind of *Twilight*

werewolf. Billy." Mills laughs and I smile back. "It wasn't funny at the time," I point out.

"So what was his tongue like? And, yes, I do mean Seth's, not Billy's. Soft or hard?"

"Mills!"

"Come on. I really want to know. I *need* to know. I'd tell *you*."

I sigh. She's right; she most certainly would. Probably more than I actually wanted to hear. Mills is a details girl. "You'd better not tell anyone else," I say.

"'Course not."

"His tongue was softish but firm. And warm, not hot."

"Was there saliva everywhere?"

"No, there wasn't. It's not like that. You make it sound gross."

"Did he poke his tongue in and out? Sophie said that's how you do it."

Funnily enough, Clover did say that that's a very common misconception. The in-out style of tonsil hockey is the sign of a rank amateur, she explained, as is the "roundy-roundy" washing machine technique. Apparently, what you're aiming for is lots of different kinds of tongue and lip action, with varying pressure.

Clover told me to imagine that kissing is an

assortment of candy. Some kisses should be rich and smooth like dark chocolate, others mellow and soft like caramel, with some twisting Twizzlers and tongue-cracking Pop Rocks thrown in for variety: all different, all sweet, all desirable. Unfortunately, because of Billy, I only tasted ordinary old milk chocolate this time.

"Sophie doesn't know what she's on about. That lizard-tongue thing is the sign of a rank amateur," I say confidently, repeating Clover's words.

Mills's eyes widen. "How *do* you kiss, then?"

"You press your lips together gently yet firmly and caress his tongue with yours. And you have to make sure that your teeth don't clink together." I blush, remembering the end-of-term party. It was the first time Seth and I kissed properly — and, put it this way, it wasn't a complete success. Thinking about it still makes me cringe.

Mills sniggers.

I swat her with a T-shirt. "Stop being such a baby."

"Sorry, sorry." She's still giggling. "But you sound so funny. Like something from a book."

I look at her. "What kind of books have you been reading?"

"Harlequin romances," she admits. "Mum keeps all the ones she's read in a box under the stairs. They're brilliant. The last one was called *Claimed by the Millionaire Bad Boy* or something like that. I'll lend you one if you like. They're full of caressing tongues and heaving bussoons."

"Bussoons?"

"You know, boobs."

I grin. "Bosoms, you eejit."

Just then, Mum runs through the door again, eyes flashing, hands balled by her sides. Her hair is pulled back off her flushed face and tied with one of Evie's white cotton bibs. She opens her hands and wipes them on her jeans, leaving vivid red marks on the faded denim. "Amy, you must have finished by now. Alex has just poured an entire pot of raspberry jam over his head. Can you give him a bath? Otherwise, I'm in danger of committing infanticide."

Mills looks at me, puzzled.

"Child murder," I tell her, standing up. "Namely, Alex. My darling brother."

Alex is nineteen months' worth of terror and devastation wrapped up in a package of Nordic blond hair and chubby cheeks. He was born on October 30, the day before Halloween, which in his case is utterly appropriate. No witch or ghoulie could cause as much trouble as Alex.

Mum shakes her head, and a plop of jam falls

onto the carpet. She whips a tissue from her pocket and dabs ineffectually at the mark. She looks as if she's about to cry.

Mum can be a bit fragile at times, what with the lack of sleep on account of Evie, who's an insomniac, and Alex, who's hyperactive even for a toddler, so I say, "Don't worry about it, Mum. The carpet's wrecked anyway. No one will notice."

She puts her face in her hands and gives a loud roar, like a lion. She's clearly losing it. "Why did I ever agree to this stupid shared holiday? The packing alone . . . I'm on the verge of a nervous breakdown."

"I think I'd better go." Mills edges toward the door.

I think Mum frightens her sometimes. Her own mum, Sue, is so sensible. She wears flowery Cath Kidston aprons and bakes.

"Have a nice holiday, Amy," Mills adds, and blows me a kiss.

"I'll try. And don't forget to e-mail me as soon as you get to Miami."

"I will. *Adiós, amiga.*"

"Mills, Miami isn't in South America. They do speak English."

"It's so far south, it's practically Mexico," she says — a little too smugly for my liking. "And loads of Cubans live there. My guidebook says it has an amazing climate, always hot. And the Costigans have a pool."

"Well, *arriba, arriba* for you," I say grimly.

Does she have to keep going on about Miami? I'm so jealous I can taste it. And envy does not taste like any kind of candy — more like battery acid.

♥ Chapter 4

BANG! BANG! BANG!

I nearly jump out of my skin. It's Saturday morning and someone is practically breaking the loo door down. I scramble around, throwing the metal teaspoon and plastic Winnie the Pooh eggcup into the medicine cabinet over the sink.

"Amy, what are you doing in there?" Mum screeches through the door. "Are you on drugs?"

"Get real — this isn't a *CSI: Miami* set, Mother. Can't I have some privacy?"

"No! We should have left for Cork two hours ago, and I still haven't packed the babies' wash things. You need to let me in there."

"I'll be out in a second, OK?"

"I hope you haven't stunk the place up. Dave's always—"

"Jeez, Mum. I really don't want to know. I'm just peeing. Is that all right? Am I allowed to pee in my own house?" I can feel my voice tightening. "Just give me one more minute and the bathroom's all yours. I'll even strap the babies into their car seats for you."

"Thanks, Amy. That would be a great help."

I hear her walk away. Strapping the babies in is no joke—Alex hates his car seat and screams and fights like a grizzly bear—but it's worth it to get rid of her. The lock on the door is wonky, and if Mum had forced her way in and found out what I'm really up to, I'd never have lived it down.

The truth is I've been conducting scientific tests on sanitary towels and tampons. Hence the teaspoon and eggcup. I've discovered that the average mini tampon can easily take a teaspoon of liquid—in this case, water colored with green food dye from the kitchen. The dye is way out of date (like most things in the baking cupboard), but I wanted my experiments to look authentic, and I couldn't find any red.

It was Clover who inspired me. Last night I couldn't sleep, so I read the latest *Goss* magazine, including Clover's agony aunt pages. One of them hit a nerve.

Dear Clover,

I have a question. I'm thirteen and I haven't started my period yet. Is there something wrong with me? I'm starting to get seriously worried. Maybe all the blood is stuck inside me. Will I get an infection? What if it comes out when I'm swimming?

All the other girls in my class talk about their period pains and stuff and I feel like such a reject. Can you help me?

Cathy in Malahide

Underneath, Clover had responded:

Dear Cathy,

Thanks for your letter. Please try not to worry. A lot of thirteen-year-olds and even older girls won't have gotten their period yet. It's perfectly normal. Before you start, your breasts may start growing and you may get hair under your arms and between your legs.

If these things have happened and you still haven't started your period by the time you are fourteen or fifteen, mention it to your mum, and she might bring you to your GP for a checkup.

I know you like swimming and are worried that you might start bleeding when you are in the water, but you will probably get some warning. Most people get only a light bleed in the first few months, just enough to stain their knickers — maybe as little as a teaspoonful of blood during the day. It might be brown or red; everyone's different.

Your period will also probably be irregular at first, so don't worry if you skip a month in the early days. And pay no attention to the girls in your class; it doesn't make them any more grown up or any cooler just because they got their period. Everyone's body is different.

Carry some sanitary pads or tampons with you in a little makeup bag so you don't worry about being caught out. And you never know, your little kit might help a friend who's just started too.

Being a girl can be a funny old business, so it's always good to be prepared and to talk to your friends or your mum about your feelings. And remember, I'm always here if you have any more questions.

Take care,

Clover XXX

Anyway, I feel a bit better about being practically the last girl in the class to start her period after reading Clover's reply. Plus, my quick experiment has proved that tampons and pads can take quite a bit of liquid, which is also reassuring. But now there's a pale green ring around the sink, from wringing everything out. I'd better clean it up before Mum starts to wonder. And what on earth am I going to do with the soggy evidence?

I look around the bathroom. Aha, nappy bags. I roll the tampons up tightly in the wet sani pads before wrapping everything in a clean, dry nappy and putting the whole lot in an apricot-colored nappy bag.

Slipping out of the bathroom, I run into my bedroom and immediately zip the nappy bag up in my sports bag. I'll sneak it outside to the bin later. Too risky right now.

Mum appears on the landing. She's like the Gestapo (the Nazi secret police) sometimes: creeping around, waiting to catch me out.

"Amy? Can you find Alex for me? He's hiding in the garden. Evie's in the car with Dave." She pushes wisps of hair back off her face. "Ten minutes till departure."

Mum always does this departure countdown thing, like the astronauts at NASA but more vocal. By the time she gets to "TWO MINUTES" and "ONE MINUTE AND COUNTING," the whole road can hear her.

We pass on the stairs and, yes, she looks completely frazzled. And she's still in her stripy blue-and-white pajamas. Oops!

"Yes, and I'll put him in the car like I said," I promise, and she smiles at me gratefully. Or it could be a wince. Probably a wince.

Alex is filthy. I find him sitting behind the shed in a pile of old potato peelings, tea bags, and worms. He's managed to drag the lid off Mum's wormery and is sifting through the rotting vegetables, using his hands as spades. He's eating what looks like a browning spiral of apple peel. At least it's not a worm.

"Alex!" I say sharply.

He drops the apple peel and gives me a toothy grin, then scrambles around and picks up a worm. "Ta, ta," he says, handing it to me.

"Yuck, Alex." I grab his chubby wrist and jiggle the worm out of his fingers. Then I pick him up under his arms so he's facing away from me and give him a good brush-down. "You are such a gross little troll." I put him down and start to brush the worst of the gunk off his jeans.

There's a worm crawling along the top of his shoe; I flick it off with my finger and resolve to scrub my hands with antibacterial soap ASAP, before its worm slime poisons my epidermis. (That's the top layer of your skin. As I might like to be a writer or a journalist, I'm trying to stretch my vocab. Clover's idea.)

I plonk Alex in the swing, pull the safety strap across his waist, and fasten it. He's not amused and kicks and wails, but I just ignore him. I try to tidy the wormery up with one of Mum's gardening trowels: I scoop up most of her precious tiger worms and plop them back inside, then put the lid back on.

It's not perfect — there are still bits of rotting carrot and apple cores littered around the garden — but it'll do. If I tell Mum, she'll probably fall to her knees and start crying — she's in enough of a state as it is.

"TWO MINUTES TILL DEPARTURE!" Mum has stuck her head out of her bedroom window and is staring at me. "What's he doing in the swing, Amy? There's no time for playing with him. And what's that in his hair?"

I look over. A plump tiger worm is wriggling down his forehead. "Just a leaf," I say, pulling it off and pitching it into the flower bed.

I lift Alex out of the swing and wash his hands in the kitchen sink, using loads of blue antibacterial soap from the squirty dispenser. I then hold him in place by wrapping both my legs around his waist in a kind of wrestler's tummy lock while I scrub my own hands. And then, finally, I carry him out through the front door under one arm, his legs kicking like a rodeo pony.

I thrust him at Dave, who's reading the paper in the front seat. "He's all yours. I've just pulled him out of the wormery. Don't tell Mum."

Dave folds up his paper, sighing. "He stinks, Amy. Get him another pair of trousers, will you?"

"I don't think it's his trousers," I say ominously.

After Alex has been changed into a fresh nappy and a new pair of trousers, we finally pull out of Sycamore Park, two hours and fifteen minutes late. I'm already exhausted. Some holiday this is turning out to be.

♥ Chapter 5

At Abbeyleix, halfway between Dublin and Cork, the car starts to feel a little funny, lopsided — like a funfair ride.

Dave swears under his breath, signals, and pulls over.

Twenty minutes later, I'm still standing on the side of the road, holding Alex's fishing rod, surrounded by bags and his large red beach bucket. Mum's walking Evie in her pram, and Alex is in his car seat, gurgling away to himself and flinging popcorn around. There's so much popcorn in the air, it looks as if it's snowing. The car has a flat tire, and guess where the spare is. You've got it — in the boot . . . underneath all the bags.

Dave's levering the car up with a jack. Beads of sweat are popping out on his forehead, and he doesn't look happy. "Bloody car," he keeps muttering. It's an old racing-green Volvo station wagon that his sister, Prue, passed on when she got her BMW SUV. The color is the only racy thing about it.

Before the babies, Dave owned a small white MG sports car. He's never liked the Volvo. He told Mum he's buying a new sports car as soon as he sells a song. Mum said she wasn't holding her breath — which was a bit mean. Dave's rock songs for toddlers are getting better, but he does need to work on his lyrics. "I'm a big green dinosaur. Hear me roar" isn't exactly Bob Dylan.

I hear a beep and look over. A metallic-blue Subaru Impreza flies past, its windows open, loud dance music blaring out, and its elephant's trunk of an exhaust roaring. As it pulls alongside, one of the boy racers inside leans out of the front passenger window and says, "You won't catch anything there. Try the River Shannon." He hoots with laughter and high-fives the boy in the back, who looks about eighteen and has a bleached mullet and orange-tinted sunglasses. Then I'm hit in the face by a shower of greasy crisps. Smelly cheese-and-onion ones too. Disgusting!

They beep and wave at me before powering away in a stink of toxic exhaust fumes.

I shake off the crisps, furious and mortified. I have nowhere to hide; I'm stuck, hemmed in by the sea of bags, forced to stand there like an idiot, my cheeks flaming. A second later I hear another beep. What now?

A red Mini Cooper pulls up behind our car and out steps Clover. She's wearing tiny white shorts, a white tank over a turquoise bikini top, and a white velour Juicy hoodie. As always, she looks fab. "Hey, Beanie — what's up?"

"Flat tire," I say miserably.

"Bummer. Hey, girlfriend," she adds in a Texan drawl, "wanna ride with me?" She blows a big pink bubble with her chewing gum and pops it, then peels the thin layer of gum off her cheeks with her fingers.

I grin at her. My day has just started to look a whole heap better.

♥ Chapter 6

Soon we're flying down the N8 in Clover's Mini Cooper, next stop Cork city.

"Can we the take the top down?" I ask eagerly.

"Later," Clover assures me. "First you promised you'd help me perfect my interview technique, and you won't be able to hear my killer questions if the roof's off. You're Efa Valentine, OK, Beanie? And if you don't know the answer, just make something up."

"We're hardly twins," I point out. I look in the mirror of the lowered sun visor and stretch the skin beside my eyes with my fingers, so I look like a cat.

Efa is tall and willowy, with a little elflike face, wispy blond hair, and these amazing chocolate-brown, almond-shaped eyes. I think her mum's

Polish or Russian or something, which would account for her exotic looks.

"And she has an American accent," I add. "I heard her on the radio recently. She does all her voice training in New York."

"Just do your best." Clover coughs and then scrunches her shoulders up and down, rolling them backward a few times, preparing herself. "Hello, Efa, I'm Clover from the *Goss* magazine. Thanks so much for giving me this interview."

I giggle. I can't help it; Clover sounds so funny.

"Beanie! Please take this seriously. I only have a few days to prepare."

"Sorry, sorry." I sit up and try to concentrate, digging my nails into my palm to stop myself from laughing. "Hi, Clover," I say, "it's lovely to meet you. I'm a big fan of the *Goss*."

"You read it?"

"Of course, religiously. I bring it on set with me all the time."

"I'm so thrilled you like it. We must give you a free subscription."

"Cool — thanks, Clover. Can I get one too? Me, Amy, I mean?"

"You're Efa, remember? Stay in character. So, Efa,"

she continues, "it must be hard to be a normal teenager, with all the films and parties and everything. Do you have a boyfriend?"

"Clover! Isn't that a bit personal?"

"Not at all. My editor wants the interview to speak to fellow teens. That's the angle. *Life as a normal teenager.* She said the boyfriend question is crucial. It's what every reader really wants to know. Anyway, I'm sure film stars are used to being asked all kinds of personal things."

I fold my arms across my chest. "Well, if I was Efa, I wouldn't be very impressed. Your approach isn't exactly subtle, is it? You should ask about her career first — how she got into acting. Make her feel comfortable. Then she might talk to you about boyfriends and stuff."

Clover is silent for a bit. Oops, maybe I've offended her. Eventually she says, "You're right, Beanie. Why didn't I think of that? I clearly need to do a lot more work on my approach and questions." She yawns. "*Siúcra ducra*, I'm pooped. It's such a long way. And I wish these saps would stop hogging the road." She nods at a familiar blue car in front of us that is weaving around like Alex on his tricycle.

It's the Crisp Criminals. I cringe and wiggle down in my seat.

"Hang on, look at that exhaust," Clover says. "It's smoking like burned toast. There must be something wrong with their engine." She pulls out into the middle of the road and peers through her windscreen at the front of the other car. "Aha. I thought so: their bonnet's smoking too. I bet they've blown a gasket."

I have no idea what she's on about, but she's right about the smoke; there are thin wafts of it coming from their bonnet. They don't seem to have noticed — or else they're stubbornly ignoring it and refusing to stop.

Clover nips back in behind them and beeps, waving at them to pull over. The boy in the backseat looks around, then makes a rude gesture with his arms and waggles his tongue at us.

"Yuck! What an evil leprechaun of a boy," Clover says. She grips the wheel and checks her rearview mirror. "If they won't budge, I'm going to overtake them. Hang on to your hat, Beanie." She presses her foot down on the accelerator, signals, and powers off, leaving the blue car in her wake.

I stick my head out the window and wave at the three boys.

"Do you know them?" Clover asks.

"Not exactly. They threw crisps at me when Dave was changing the tire."

"I wondered what the smell was, but I didn't want to say anything."

"Clover! I hope you'd tell me if I had BO or doggy breath or something."

She laughs. "'Course I would. I'll give them crisps, cheeky monkeys." She reaches over and pulls something red out of her handbag, which is lodged beneath my seat, and tosses it out the window. It sails along in the air for a moment before slapping against their windscreen. "I'll see your crisps, boys," she yells, "and I'll raise you a *Goss* special!"

The boys screech to a halt, peel something off the glass, and stare after us in disbelief, their mouths wide open.

"What *was* that?" I ask as we zip away. The boys are now ants in the distance.

"An edible bra. I was going to give it to Sylvie for a laugh. There's still a box of them in the office. They're made of this gross chewy stuff — they use it to make edible cards for dogs."

I stare at her in amazement. The mind boggles. "But what are they for? The edible bras, I mean."

"Valentine's Day. I included them in my 'Original Presents for the Boy Who Floats Your Boat' roundup."

What can you say to that?

Clover flicks on her iPod speakers and Avril Lavigne's voice rings out. "Remember this one, Bean Machine?" she says, belting out the chorus of "Girl-friend" while jiggling her upper body to the music and tapping the steering wheel with her left hand.

We steam on along the N8.

"Having fun yet?" she asks me when the song ends.

"I would be if I didn't stink of cheese and onion."

"Here." She reaches into her handbag again and pulls out a chunky glass bottle. Old Rose by Jo Malone, one of Clover's prized possessions. "Just one spritz, mind," she warns. "I have to smell lush for Brains."

"Thanks, Clover." I put on my best American accent. "I love you, man."

"Don't blame you." She grins at me. "I'm pretty cute." Then she signals left and pulls onto the gravel shoulder with a squeal of tires. "Now, let's get the top down, Beanie. West Cork, here we come."

♥ Chapter 7

Clover stops at a garage in Skibbereen to wait for Dave, as the directions to Haven House — the place we're staying in — are pretty complicated. Following him out of town, we drive down a small wiggling road, lined with bushy hedgerows, and through the pretty Lough Ine village — which is basically a pub painted tea-rose pink and a small ice-cream-shop/post-office — until we reach a large lake. After another minute or so, we pull up beside a small stone harbor surrounded by mossy old trees, their leaves suspended just over the water.

There are all kinds of boats bobbing on the lake — orange kayaks, old blue pedal boats with broken seats, yachts, and lots of brightly painted wooden fishing boats with engines on the back. It's so beautiful, it looks like a picture postcard.

We get out and stand beside Mum and Dave by the harbor edge. Evie and Alex are both asleep in the car. Alex looks as if he's been let loose in Willy Wonka's Chocolate Factory; there's a melty brown ring around his mouth, and the front of his hair is brown, too.

"How was your trip?" Clover asks Mum.

Mum shakes her head. "Don't ask. Alex only fell asleep about ten minutes ago. If I ever have to listen to his nursery-rhyme CD again, I swear I'll shoot myself. Five hours of 'The Wheels on the Bus Go Round and Round.' Aagh!"

Clover smiles gently. "We're here now."

"But where's *here*?" Mum looks at Dave, who is gazing out at the water. "Dave, where's the house? It's not that one, is it?" She points at a white mansion with rows and rows of tall glass-paned windows.

Dave shakes his head. "No, it's over there." He nods at a green patch in the middle of the lake.

Clover squints. "Isn't that an island?"

Dave nods eagerly and grins. "Yes. Isn't it cool?"

"An island?" Mum narrows her eyes. "You never said anything about an island, Dave." She doesn't look happy.

"It's a surprise," Dave says, the smile quickly dropping off his face. "Art thought it would be exciting. Romantic."

(Dad booked the house — he's a bit of a control freak.)

"Romantic? With all the baby gear?" Mum demands. "Is he deranged? I can't believe you didn't warn me." She glares at him. "Tell me there's a car ferry."

Dave gives a hollow laugh. "Don't be silly, Sylvie. There are only two houses on the island. We have our own boat. Two of them, in fact." He gestures at the steps leading down to the water, and sure enough, a yellow fishing boat is tied to the railing. "The other one must be on the island with Prue and her lot. And there's a private beach only three minutes' walk from the house."

Prue is Dave's posh big sister. Her ferry arrived in Rosslare at six this morning. Dad and Shelly are following us down next week. Shelly has a hospital appointment on Monday, so it will be Tuesday before they get here. It's a miracle they are joining us at all. Mum and Dad only started speaking to each other again a few weeks ago, after Dad "forgot" to tell Mum about his and Shelly's secret wedding in Barbados.

Oh, and that Shelly's expecting a baby. They're all still a bit funny around each other.

Mum stares at the boats and then back at Dave. "And how exactly do we get the bags from the beach to the house? And if you say donkey, I'll thump you."

"Wheelbarrow," Dave admits. "Far more reliable than a donkey."

Clover and I giggle, but Mum throws us one of her wicked-fairy-from-*Sleeping-Beauty* looks, so we stop.

"David Marcus," Mum says, her voice tight and her eyes flashing. "One of these days—" She stops, puts both her hands over her face, and makes a muffled squeaking noise.

Clover pinches me and whispers excitedly, "An island! How exciting! Isn't it Fab City?"

In the end, despite Mum's reservations, the trip over to the island isn't all that bad. We load the boat up with all the bags and baby equipment, and after a quick refresher lesson from Dave, Clover helms it to the beach. She's been in and out of fishing boats all her life with Gramps, so she's pretty confident. My job is to stop Alex from jumping overboard, which takes quite an effort, as he's mad about any kind of water, especially deep water he can actually drown in.

Clover approaches the beach a little too quickly and grinds the bottom of the boat against the stony sand. It makes a sickening crunching noise, but no water comes in, so Dave says it's OK; she hasn't holed it — this time. Clover's shaken at first, but after a few seconds she bounces back.

"Hey, Beanie, look — our own private beach!" She gives me a wicked grin. "You know what that means? Topless sunbathing and skinny-dipping."

"What do you think, Sylvie? Fancy a bit of skinny-dipping later, when the kids are in bed?" Dave grins.

Mum rolls her eyes at him. "Please. We're not teenagers, Dave. And if you want to give Prue a heart attack, Clover, then going topless is a good way to go about it."

Clover isn't bothered. "Hey, Dan's a doctor, so heart attack, smart attack — he can always revive her. I for one intend to get an all-over tan."

(Dan is Prue's husband. He's a GP in Hove, where they live — which according to Dave is a posh seaside town near Brighton, England.)

Mum plays with Alex and Evie on the beach while the rest of us load up the rusty green wheelbarrows. Dave and Clover take one each and begin to push them toward the house — correction: Dave does. The wheels of Clover's keep getting stuck, and she's swearing so much that Mum says, "For goodness sake, help her, Dave. Quickly, before Alex picks up even more bad language."

When we finally get to the house — a sunny yellow two-story Georgian house with huge sash windows, ivy growing over them like wiggly eyebrows — Prue and Dan are there to greet us. Baby Bella is on Prue's hip, but there's no sign of Ollie or Denis, her boys.

Denis is a nightmare! The last time they were over, Mills and I were sunbathing in the back garden, and Denis soaked us with the hose. Another time, he squeezed his feet into Clover's favorite silver Converses so he could play soccer with Dave and Dan in the back garden, 'cause his own shoes were wet. They came back muddy and stretched. Clover wasn't impressed.

"Darling brother," Prue says, throwing her arms around Dave. "How lovely to see you. Won't this be fun?"

Dave must be smothered. I'm standing several meters away, and her musky perfume smells stronger than toilet cleaner.

Prue steps back. She's wearing beige canvas to-the-knee shorts, navy Keds, and a neatly ironed white button-up shirt. Her straight blond hair is pulled back in a navy velvet Alice band.

"I hope you don't mind, darling," she says, "but I've allocated the rooms already. I thought it would make things easier." (For someone who's Irish, Prue sounds a lot like the queen of England.)

Clover slants me a look. "Sylvie's not going to like that," she whispers.

Prue starts to show us around. "This is the Blue Bedroom, where Dan and I are sleeping," she says, waving her hands around a large room with three big sash windows, all with sea views; an enormous four-poster bed with an eggshell-blue canopy; a squashy sofa with sky-blue cushions; wall-to-wall wardrobes; and its own enormous bathroom with a power shower and whirlpool bath.

"And I thought the Yellow Bedroom might suit you and Dave, Sylvie." She swings open the door to a much smaller room down the corridor, with only one window, no sea views; a normal-size double bed; no sofa; only one small pine chest of drawers; and a tiny bathroom with a view of the sea, only if you stand on the loo seat and peer through the very small window above.

Mum doesn't say a word. She throws Dave a look, but he's studiously avoiding her gaze.

Prue gives me and Clover the Safari Room because

of the French doors, but Clover has already chris-
tened it the "Room That Taste Forgot."

"Denis isn't very good with balconies," Prue tells
us. "I'll put him in the Lilac Room until your boyfriend arrives, Clover dear."

Clover hisses in my ear, "I'm sure the spawn child
is *very* good with balconies — trying to push people
off them, that is."

I giggle into my hand.

♥ Chapter 8

As soon as Prue has skipped off, we troop downstairs to the kitchen. "It's outrageous," Mum says, propping her hip against the granite counter. Her eyes are flashing like Fourth of July fireworks. "Prue gets"—she counts on her fingers—"a whirlpool bath, a sea view, and a four-poster bed. What do I get? A sickly yellow room, that's what. And rubbish white curtains that let the light in. The room's so small, Evie's crib will just fit beside our bed, but we'll have to put Alex's portable crib in the bathroom. Which means I won't even get one flaming bath in the evening. All I wanted was a bit of peace and quiet and the occasional bath."

Dave looks confused. "Sylvie, I think you're over-reacting. You can have your bath during the day. And the room's the same color as our bedroom at home. You like yellow; you think it's calming."

Hot red spots appear on Mum's cheeks. "We're on holiday," she hisses. "I wanted a change. Not the same. Something different! Why did *she* get to pick the rooms? Tell me that!" She thrusts her hands on her hips.

Dave seems a bit alarmed, and I can't say I blame him. Mum looks like a volcano about to erupt. She's pacing the kitchen tiles, her lips pressed together, hard.

Just then Prue skips into the kitchen. (Can the woman not walk like normal mortals?) Unlike Mum, she looks calm and happy, with baby Bella balanced on her hip and a jaunty red-and-white-polka-dot nappy bag slung over her shoulder. "Hello, all," she trills, tinkling her fingers at us. "Just making Bella a little snack. Does Evie-Deevie like organic rice cakes and carrot sticks? Carrots are so good for their teeth, don't you think?"

Mum opens her mouth to say something, but before she gets a chance, Prue adds, "I've already stocked the fridge, Sylvie, so there's no need to worry. Now, I don't let my three near processed food or sugar." She shudders and makes a funny face, as if she's constipated, and I try not to laugh. "So it's porridge for breakfast," she continues. "I'm sure little Evie loves porridge, don't you, angel?"

She crouches down and puts her finger out to stroke Evie's cheek — but Evie's too quick for her and gives it a little nip with her teeth.

Prue squeals and jumps back in fright, knocking over the trash bin with a clatter and almost dropping Bella.

Evie starts to wail. Mum picks her up and jiggles her around on her hip, but she won't stop. She's like a little fire engine.

Mum sighs. "I'll just take Evie for a little walk around the garden to calm her down. And, Prue, I'm sorry, but I can't stand porridge. I'm more of a Sugar Puffs girl myself." She gives a tight smile. "And, I agree, there's far too much sugar and salt in processed foods, but frankly, I don't care. I'm on holiday and I plan to spend as little time as possible cooking. My lot will happily eat beans and sausages every day, so don't worry about them. They won't starve. And, by the way, congratulations on bagging the biggest room for yourself. Way to go, Prue."

Prue gasps but Mum ignores her and marches outside with a still bawling Evie in her arms. Prue puts Bella into a high chair, then folds her arms across her chest. "Well," she says in a breathy voice, staring at Dave; her eyebrows are so high they're almost halfway up her forehead.

Clover hops up onto the counter, dangling her brown legs (fake-baked only last night, she told me in the car) and yawning. "Any chocolate or Coke, Dave? My blood sugar's all over the place."

Prue's eyebrows rise even farther.

Dave just smiles. "Nope. Fancy a shopping trip later? Amy can go with you to help, if she likes."

Clover's eyes light up. "Can we use the boat on our own?"

"Yep."

"Excellent." She puts her hand up to high-five me. "You on, Beanie?"

"You bet."

Half an hour after Mum and Prue's encounter in the kitchen, Mum still isn't back from walking Evie. Dave is starting to fret. He's already searched the whole house for them.

Clover is lying on the sun lounger, lapping up the rays, Alex is napping in his new bathroom/nursery, and Prue's stooped over some sort of evil-smelling bean-and-vegetable concoction on the Aga, like a witch stirring a cauldron. I keep half expecting her to start chanting "Double, double, toil and trouble" like one of the old hags in *Macbeth*. I caught her stroking the Aga earlier — which is weird behavior, if you ask me. Bella is sitting on a rug at Prue's feet, chewing away happily on a cardboard copy of *The Very Hungry Caterpillar*.

Dan is outside, watching Ollie and Denis on the trampoline. Denis is larger than the average nine-year-old (he's the size of a small mountain!), so poor old Ollie, who's small for three, is being boinged all over the place. Every now and then Denis suddenly stops jumping, making Ollie land awkwardly and wail in protest. No wonder Dan's watching them so intently.

As everyone else is busy, I offer to help look for Mum. There's no sign of her in the garden, so I megaphone my hands and roar, "Mum!" at the top of my voice.

Still nothing.

Then I hear a creaking noise to my right and notice a gap in the ivy-covered wall. A tall, dark-haired boy of about fifteen or sixteen walks through the old metal gateway, a green canvas sack slung over his back, a black-and-white dog at his heels. Through the gate behind him, I spot a hedge.

The boy dumps the contents of the sack into a wheelbarrow by the wall and wipes his hands on the front of his cutoff jeans. The dog waits obediently by his side. The boy lifts his head. "Lost yer mam?" he asks with a strong West Cork lilt.

He's so good-looking, my breath catches and I blush instantly. Unable to speak, I nod wordlessly, just gawking at him. I can't help it. His face is nutty brown, and he has intense, hypnotic eyes, the color of a stormy sea — a swirl of green, blue, and gunmetal gray. I can feel my blood racing through my veins and, *thud-thud-thud*, my heart pumping in my chest.

He's not wearing a top, and his broad, tanned chest is all sweaty and heaving, his arms strong and muscular. Judging by the tan on his legs, he must wear shorts all the time. His nose has a distinct bump, and his jeans are grass-stained, but, be still my swooning heart, he certainly has . . . something.

"She blond? Carrying a baby?" he continues.

I nod again.

"Down there." He jabs a thumb toward the sea. "On the beach."

"Um, thanks," I manage.

"No bother." He walks back through the gate toward the hedge. Looking closer, I see there's a gap in it. Then it comes to me — it's not a hedge at all; it's a maze. Wow! How cool!

I'm about to go and investigate when I hear Dan call from the garden. "Amy!"

Reluctantly I turn toward his voice, the strange boy's face still swimming in front of my eyes.

♥ Chapter 9

The following morning I'm sitting on the patio with Clover. I didn't get much sleep last night. Clover snored all night, like a slobbery dog with adenoid problems, and I'm hoping to have a nice snooze in the sun after breakfast. The sky is cornflower blue, with only a few high, wispy clouds, and we've already planned to cut loose from the noisy babies and their even noisier mums and hit the beach later.

It's a bit nippy to be eating outside, but we're avoiding the mayhem in the kitchen. We picked up our cereal bowls and skedaddled just after Mum and Prue launched into a heated argument about television watching during mealtimes.

It's their second disagreement of the morning, and it's not even nine o'clock yet. The first was over being dressed at the breakfast table. This morning Prue is once again perfectly turned out in pristine jeans with a crease ironed down the front, a crisp white shirt, and another velvet Alice band, red this time.

She insisted on her brood being washed and dressed before they ate. Mum's still in her raggedy gray pj's and pink terry-cloth robe, with wild Amy Winehouse hair. She hasn't fully woken up yet, let alone washed and dressed either herself or Alex and Evie.

They'd barely finished that argument when the great telly debate began. They're still at it. The French doors are open, and their heated voices are carrying all the way out here.

"But it rots their brains, Sylvie," Prue is saying. "And it overstimulates them. I only let my boys watch educational programs."

Through the open doorway I see Mum grab the remote off the kitchen counter and channel-hop until the *D-D-D-D-D-Dora the Explorer* theme tune rings out. "Now!" she says triumphantly. "Dora's very educational. All that Spanish and map reading."

Prue presses her lips together into a tight line and says nothing.

"Do you think they'll be bickering for the entire

holiday?" Clover asks me in a low voice, stretching her legs out in front of her and crossing them at the ankles. (We're sitting on spindly-legged metal chairs. Mine nearly froze my bum when I sat down, but it's warmed up a bit now.) Clover gives a huge yawn, and I can see her wisdom teeth. "It's very tedious," she adds, then winks. "But quite entertaining. Hey, in a mud wrestle, who would you bet on, Sylvie or Prue?"

I don't even have to think about it. "Mum! Prue would be afraid of getting filthy. And I bet she'd do that girlie slapping thing." I demonstrate for Clover, flapping my hands in the air like a seal's flippers and making high-pitched girlie squeaks.

Clover cracks up and falls over laughing. "You're probably right. But I think old Prudie has hidden depths. After all, she did shoot Denis out from between her legs. He must have been a *giant* baby."

"Clover!" I scrunch up my nose. "Do you have to be so graphic?"

"Sorry, Beans. Changing the subject, do you think Denis will break his vow of silence?"

So far Denis hasn't uttered a word — not yesterday, not this morning. Not a peep. When Clover tried tickling him earlier, to make him laugh or even just squeak, he only scowled, grunted, and squeezed her hand so tight that he nearly broke it. Then he made a rude sign with his fingers and waggled them in her face.

I snorted into my hand, and even Clover looked a bit shocked. She tried to wrestle his hand down, and of course, Prue caught her at it.

"What are you doing, Clover?" she raged.

Quick as a flash, Clover said, "Teaching Denis sign language." She crossed her hands in front of her body and tipped her hips, giving Prue a sugary sweet smile.

I laughed so much that milk went up my nose, and I spat my mouthful of Rice Krispies all over the table. I couldn't help it. You see, Alex's favorite kids' program is called "Something Special"—its smiley presenter teaches children how to sign. Clover and I were babysitting recently and watched it with him. We were trying to make Alex copy the gestures, but he was far more interested in his toy trains than the screen. Anyway, Clover has just told Denis—in sign language—to change her nappy.

"What did you just say in sign language, then?" Prue asked suspiciously, one hand on her hip, as if she were about to do "I'm a Little Teapot."

"Put on your shorts," Clover lied effortlessly before signing again. "Put on." She crossed her arms.

"Your shorts." She touched her hips. "He'll boil in those heavy cargo pants."

"That's really cool, Clover," Mum said, genuinely impressed. "I didn't know you could sign."

Prue just sucked in her cheeks. I don't think she's taken to Clover.

"Do I look like I've got the plague?" Clover asks. She's stuck soggy Rice Krispies all over her face. She puts her hands out in front of her like a zombie, closes her eyes, and moans like one of the evil undead.

"Hello! Anyone home?" A singsong voice suddenly pierces the air. A girl a few years older than Clover is walking toward us. She has a short crop of hair, the color of blackberries. A stocky gray Labrador with a bit of a limp is following closely behind her. When I look at his bright, loyal eyes, I think of our old dog, Timmy. He was a black Lab too. He died just after Mum and Dad's separation. Great timing. I was devastated. First my gran died, then my parents split up, then Timmy died — bang, bang, bang, one after the other — and my whole life came tumbling down, like a run of dominoes. If it wasn't for Clover and Mills, and Mum, I suppose, I would have gone crazy. I still miss Gran and Timmy.

"Hi there." The girl smiles, coming to a stop in front of me and Clover, her friendly garnet-blue eyes crinkling at the corners. She's staring at Clover's face, but is clearly too polite to say anything about Clover's disfiguring skin disease.

Clover wipes the cereal off with the back of her hand. It drops to the floor, and the dog starts to wolf it down.

"Dante!" The girl pulls him back by his collar. "Bad boy."

Clover laughs. "It's only Rice Krispies."

"Oh, ay? Good for the skin, is it? Like a face mask?" the girl asks.

"Something like that. I'm Clover, by the way. And this is my niece Amy. We're staying here for two weeks. Do you live on the island?"

"Ah, no. More's the pity. Beautiful, isn't it?" She waves her hand around the garden. "I live on the Baltimore Road. Sorry, I'm Martie. I look after Haven House for Esther; she owns the place."

"Does Esther have a son?" I ask. I'm dying to find out more about the boy from the maze.

Martie shakes her head. "No. Why?"

"There was a boy here yesterday. With a dog."

She looks at me for a moment, as if deciding what to say. "That would be Kit Harper. He's the gardener. He wasn't rude to you, was he?"

"What? No. Not at all. Didn't say much, really."

"That'd be Kit all right." She smiles gently. "Best left to his own devices." She sighs. "We've had a few complaints about him from the people renting Haven. Nothing serious. But some people around here think he's trouble."

I can almost see Clover's ears prick up at the word *trouble*.

"But he's a brilliant gardener, that's for sure," Martie continues. "The place has never looked better. Esther has a bit of a soft spot for him. Says he's —" She stops as Gramps walks out through the French doors.

"There you are, girls," he says. "It's like World War III in there, so I thought I'd join you."

Gramps drove down on his own late last night to avoid the traffic. I think he was also trying to avoid being lumped with either Alex or Evie; there was talk of separating them to make the trip easier for Mum and Dave, but in the end it didn't happen. Much as Gramps loves his youngest grandchildren, he likes peace and quiet while he's driving.

"Hello." He puts out his hand politely to Martie. "I'm Len Wildgust. Clover's dad and Amy's grampa."

Martie shakes it heartily. "Martie Coghill."

Gramps stares at her, still gripping her hand. "Did you say *Coghill*, my dear?"

She nods and smiles. "That's right. It's a funny name, isn't it? My family came from England originally."

Gramps realizes he's still clutching her hand and lets it go gently. "You don't know an Esther Coghill, by any chance?"

Martie nods. "Aye, Esther's my nan. Owns this place, in fact. Lived here for years with my grandad before he died. She moved off the island a few years back, when it got too much for her. Not that she'd admit it, of course. I've taken over most of the rental work, but she still deals with the bookings and the paperwork."

Gramps staggers a little and then sits down on a chair beside me. He looks very shaken. "Esther," he whispers. "Fancy that."

"Do you know Nan?" Martie asks him.

"Was her maiden name Smylie?"

Martie nods. "That's right."

"Then I do." He smiles softly. "I met her when she was nursing up in Dublin. She was my first love."

Clover gasps and nudges me with her elbow. "Are you thinking what I'm thinking?" she whispers.

"Operation Emma?" I whisper back.

She looks at me blankly.

"Jane Austen," I add.

Still nothing. She clearly doesn't know her Austen very well. If she did, she'd know that Emma Wood-house was one of Austen's best-ever heroines. Much more interesting than those drippy Bennet girls from *Pride and Prejudice*. Emma was a matchmaker. It all went a bit wrong in the end, but her heart was in the right place.

"Operation matchmaker!" I hiss back.

Clover grins. "My thoughts exactly, Beanie."

♥ Chapter 10

"Gramps hasn't seen his sisters for more than forty years. Isn't that amazing?" Clover stops, puts a hand on my shoulder, lifts her flip-flop, and shakes it. A pebble plops out, and we start walking again. The sun is shining and we're on our way to one of the island's private beaches.

"I think it's kind of sad," I say. "And the whole business with Esther is sad too."

As soon as Martie left, Gramps told us the whole story. He met Esther Smylie forty years ago at a tea dance at the Royal Marine Hotel in Dun Laoghaire. She was there with a gang of nurses from the Adelaide Hospital, and he was at a farewell celebration. His twin sisters, Mabel and Tully, were emigrating to Australia; he hasn't seen them since. After that night,

Gramps and Esther dated for a while before it all went wrong.

"Should we ring Esther now?" I say. "See if she'll go for dinner with Gramps?"

"I'm not sure, Beanie. They parted on pretty bad terms. She might not be all that impressed with the idea."

"She can't still be angry after all this time, surely?"

She shrugs. "Some people hold grudges all their life. And Gramps did stand her up on a date. . . . Maybe this isn't such a good idea."

"He just got the time wrong."

Clover sucks in her breath and shakes her head. "But she waited for more than an hour. In the pouring rain. And then he disappeared for a week without any real explanation."

"For work! And that's not true, anyway; he left her a message. And he went to the hospital to see her the minute he got back from his trip — she refused even to speak to him! It wasn't *all* his fault, Clover. She's equally to blame."

"Maybe," she says slowly. But after a moment, she hands me her mobile. "Go for it, Beanie."

I find the yellow sticky note in my pocket and tap in Esther's number. It was rather conveniently written in the house's big blue folder of instructions. Clover leans right in so she can eavesdrop.

"Hello?" a woman's voice answers.

"Hi, Mrs. Coghill. My name's Amy Green, and I'm staying in Haven House with my family."

"Hello, my dear. And do call me Esther. Anything wrong? Water hasn't gone off again, has it?"

"Oh, no, nothing like that. This might seem a bit out of the blue, but we were talking to Martie earlier, and it turns out that Gramps — sorry, my grampa — knows you. He's staying with us. He got chatting to Martie, who mentioned your name, and he remembered you from years back. . . ." I pause and take a breath. "Len Wildgust?"

I wait for Esther to say something. Finally she says, "Len, eh? Now, there's a blast from the past." She gives a short laugh. "What a coincidence. I can't believe _Len's_ staying on the island."

I take another deep breath. "Gramps, sorry, _Len_ would love to see you again, Mrs. Coghill — I mean, Esther."

"Would he, now? . . . Well, why not? I'd love to catch up with him. He always was such a tonic. And a very accomplished dancer. Would he like to come over for tea? Or maybe something stronger? Does he like sloe gin? I make my own."

"How about dinner in Skibbereen?" I suggest. "Thursday night? Around eight?"

"Perfect. But he must come here, Autumn Cottage. I insist. I'll cook up something very special. Martie can give him directions. She's up at the house most mornings, talking to the gardener. But I have to ask, my dear, why is it you ringing and not Len?"

"He was a bit nervous," I say, not wanting to give away how much I know. "He hasn't been on a date since my granny died."

"A date?" She laughs. "Oh, my. No wonder he's nervous. . . . Thursday it is. Tell Len I'll see him then."

I click the mobile off.

"Yeah!" Clover says, clapping her hands together and doing a little wiggly dance. "Way to go. Gramps has a hot date. And speaking of 'hot,' I've been dying to know all morning—what does he look like? Kitty Kit. The one who's trouble." She puts on a dramatic deep voice when she says "trouble," like someone from a movie trailer.

"Utter Swoonsville," I admit. There's no point trying to hide things from Clover. She'll see him herself soon enough, anyway. "Black hair, tanned. Amazing body."

"Do I detect a mini crush?"

"Not at all." I try not to sound too defensive. I had a dream about him last night. He was running with his dog on the beach. Then the dog turned into Billy, Seth's dog, and Kit turned into Seth. It was all very weird.

Clover chuckles. "I'm only teasing. I know you're hopelessly devoted to Sethy baby. But it's an added bonus having a bit of eye candy in the garden, don't you think? *Très Desperate Housewives.*"

We reach the beach and lie down on our towels to soak up the sun. I close my eyes and wonder what Seth's up to in Rome right at this minute. I'm starting to miss him.

♥ Chapter 11

On Tuesday afternoon, there's a letter waiting for me on the kitchen table. It's from Seth; I'd recognize his sprawling handwriting anywhere. I rip open the plump-as-a-pillow envelope, and small black razor-thin stones fall onto my lap. I pick them up and pile them on the table in front of me, where they wink in the light. Then I pull out a crumpled browning leaf and two squashed and bruised white flower heads.

The letter is on white paper with a torn, wiggly left-hand side, as if it's been ripped out of a note-book. I start to read:

Hey, babe,
    A little bit of Italia, just for you.
    Missing you already. It's not bad here, but a bit

Snoresville. We're staying in a villa in the hills just outside Rome. Mum is teaching twice a day, in the morning and then again in the early evening. Too hot to concentrate in the afternoon, apparently.

The olds in Polly's class are way dodgy-looking: lots of men in big baggy shorts you could hide a whole kennel of dogs in, and women in Jesus sandals with gnarly yellow toenails. There's one girl, Jin, who always wears bikini tops and rainbow tie-dyed skirts with bells on the hem that make her sound like Tinker Bell when she walks. She winked at me this morning, and she's at least seventeen! She's here with her mum.

I saw a firefly last night — amazing! Wish you'd been here to see it too: flitting around the place with its own little light source. Mad to watch.

What's the house like? Is it old and haunted? Whoooooooooooooo! (That's a ghost, by the way.)

Spookily yours,
Seth

XXXXXXXXXXXXXXXXXXXXXXXXXXXXXX
XXXXXXXXXXXXXXXXXXXXXXXXXXXXXX
XXXXXXXXXXXXXXXXXXXXXXXXXXXXXX

Tinker Bell winked at him, did she? Cheeky minx. I read the letter again. Nothing about him ignoring her. In fact, he sounds proud of himself. Yikes! She could be cheerleader material with big wobbly boobs straining out of that skimpy bikini top. For all I know, he could have winked back. Maybe he fancies her.

I throw the letter down on the table in annoyance. Then I notice a second page, peeping out from under the first, like a shy twin.

It's a poem. Written out carefully and neatly. It must have taken him ages.

For Amy
You Make Me Smile

The denim night sky stretches out in front of me,
The spikes of the stars jut into my senses.
I remember sitting under a tree, just the two of us;
I remember silence.
I remember warm arms, warm lips, warm hearts.
Oh, wrap me up in the comfort of those arms
And take me home.
I am yours
Because you make me smile.

Seth X

For a second the world stops dead; all I can hear is the sound of my own heart beating. *Thump-thump-thump*. Seth wrote a poem — for me! It's the most romantic thing that has ever happened to me in my whole entire life. I clutch the page to my chest, close my eyes, and give a big swoony sigh.

I click into my e-mail account to write back to him:

> Hi, Seth,
> Thanks for your letter; it arrived today. Super-speedy delivery. Must have cost you a fortune. I didn't know you were a poet!
> Missing you loads too. And give Tinker Bell a good slap from me.

I delete the last sentence and calm myself down. I try again.

> Probably best to steer well clear of Tinker Bell. Just in case she gets the wrong idea.
> At least it's always hot and sunny in Italy. You'll get a great tan. Clover and I were at the beach earlier, but we had to come back 'cause it started to rain. Typical!

As I write, I imagine Seth with a tan. And then my mind slips to Kit's already tanned chest. I shake my head — but Kit's handsome face is still there. I try to concentrate on Seth. Seth's smattering of freckles over his cute nose, his amazing blue eyes and the way he lets his hair flop over them when he's upset or trying to hide something. OK, I'm back on Seth-track now.

What else has happened? Nothing really. Food fight at dinner last night — Denis versus Alex. Denis won. Poor Alex didn't stand a chance. Denis fired a bread roll at him and it nearly landed in his eye, so Mum told Denis to go to his room. But Prue, my crazy aunt, said he could stay, that he didn't start it. Mum said, "But he's nine, Prue. Alex is only a baby."

It's all fun and games at Camp MadHaven, I can tell you. Mum and Prue still aren't really speaking to each other again.

The house we're staying in has its own private island with a huge garden, a beach, and even a maze — it's a*maz*ing. (Get it?) And it is kind of haunted — by the ghost of girlfriends past. Although she is very much alive.

It turns out that one of Gramps's old flames owns the place — isn't that wild? They're having dinner together and everything. I'll let you know if sixty-year-olds kiss on a first date. Yuck — on second thought, maybe I won't!

Muchos kisses and hugs,

Amy XXX

I decide three kisses is enough. One looks a bit scabby, but I don't want to go overboard. After all, he is staying in a weird commune with booby bikini girl. I have to keep him interested.

Then I spot a new e-mail from Mills:

Hello, oh, wise and wonderful friend,

Help me!!!

I've only been here two days and I'm already going insane. The Costigans are barking mad. Ria has about ten showers a day and then leaves her damp towels all over the house. Rex is never off the phone. He walks around the place jabbering away into this pop-star headset thing and waving his spade-size hands around. He loves himself too and never stops looking in the mirror! I caught him gazing at his reflection in the shiny toaster this morning.

Miami is awesome, though—so it's almost worth it.

But I have a major, huge problem. There's this boy . . .

The pool filter is broken at his family's place and the pool's full of algae, so he and his friend have been using the Costigans' pool most days. They know Ria and Rex through the movie business.

He's so gorge, Amy, and way out of my league, but I have to try. Although, so far he seems to be ignoring me.

HOW DO I MAKE HIM NOTICE ME??

How did you make Seth sit up and pay attention? I need your boy expertise, drastically. Wish you were here!

Marlon keeps asking about Clover. He wants to know if she has a serious boyfriend. I think he fancies her!!!!!!! Yuck. He's only eleven.

You must be really missing Seth. Hope you're surviving without the hot snogging?!

Your bestest, bestest friend eva,

Mills

XXX

"Oi, Beanie; what's up? Anything interesting?" Clover has come in and is peering over my shoulder. I put my hands up to cover the screen, but it's too late. Mills's question is in such huge caps, it's impossible to hide.

"*How do I make him notice me?* That would make a great Dear Clover letter, don't you think? Who's the e-mail from? Mills?"

My face drops, but I say nothing.

She grins. "So it *is* Mills."

Yikes! Mills will kill me.

Clover ruffles my hair. "Don't worry; we'll change the name and details to protect the innocent. But I think I can help her."

"You can? In that case . . ." I start to sing the dwarfs' song from *Snow White:* "Heigh-ho, heigh-ho, it's off to work we go."

Clover laughs. "Sure thing, Beanie-Dwarf."

♥ Chapter 12

Dear Celine,

How to make a boy notice you? That's an interesting one. Luckily, most males are simple creatures with simple needs.

1. **Food**
   Offer him something to eat — any kind of hot meat product is a winner: steak, hamburgers, spicy sausages. Or failing that, tortilla chips and any kind of junk food.

2. **Sports and Hobbies**
   Boys love talking about sports and their hobbies. They also love girls who will happily chow

down popcorn beside them while watching the Gunners sock it to Man City, or Munster thrashing Harlequins. If you actually like footie or rugby, even better.

But, of course, some boys are more music heads. . . .

3. Music

Boys also love to talk about music. Find out what kind of music he's into and do some research on the Internet. Tell him about a great new band you've found (a band you think he'll get — based on your research) and play him a song on your mobile. He'll be very impressed.

4. Technology

Boys like to yabber on about mobiles and the latest electronic gadgets — iPods and Apple Macs and the like. Frankly, computer speak bores me to tears. (Megabytes and memory cards, anyone?) But if it's your bag, go for it!

5. To Feel Important

All of us like to feel important, and boys are no different. By showing an interest in him at all, you are pandering to his inner "I am a god—why has no one discovered it yet?" feelings.

Tell him how amazing he is; tell him how awesome he was on the rugby pitch / on stage / in class. Everyone likes to feel special.

On a less frivolous note . . .

6. Someone to Listen

Yes, even boys need someone to talk to and, most important, to listen. Be an unjudgmental ear. Tell him, "I'm here if you ever want someone to talk to." Maybe he'll never need it, but by offering, you are showing that you care.

But enough of the touchy-feely stuff. . . .

7. Fast Cars

Boys love fast cars! The flashier the better. If you have a dad / grandad / uncle / godfather who owns a Porsche or an Aston Martin, cool. Get him to collect you from school in it. I guarantee it'll make your boy's head turn. Notice, shmotice—he won't be able to stop staring at you.

All of these tips can help, but remember: above all, the most important thing is to be yourself. Yes, show an interest in his hobbies — find out what movies and music he likes etc., etc. — but use these topics as conversation openers. Don't pretend to like horror movies if you'd rather hide under the bed than watch one. You'll be found out pretty quickly when you run screaming out of the cinema on your first date.

And finally — smile; be natural. Don't pretend to be someone you're not. Yes, boys like girls to look nice, but give him a genuine, friendly smile, and he'll choose you over the belt-for-a-skirt girl with the frown every time. Be fun, be as confident as you can, and enjoy his company. If you have to be someone you're not around him, find another boy. If he's worth dating, he'll accept and like you for who you are.

All the best,

Clover XXX

♥ Chapter 13

It's eight in the evening. The babies are all in bed — yeah! — and the parentals plus me and Clover are sitting around the wooden kitchen table after dinner. There's a deep cut in the wood — I could swear it wasn't there this morning; the gash looks clean and fresh. I wonder if Denis has been at it with his Swiss Army Knife. I spotted him playing with it on the patio earlier, cutting worms in half with its miniature scissors. Yuck! Whoever gave that demon boy a knife is deranged.

"Let's play a game of Trivial Pursuit," Prue says brightly. "It wouldn't be a proper holiday without board games."

Clover groans. She hates Trivial Pursuit. Too much like school, she says; plus it's hard to cheat. She has tried stealing the triangular pie pieces and dropping them in when no one's looking, but someone usually catches her at it.

"Trivial Pursuit might be a bit difficult for Amy," she says, throwing me a don't-say-a-word wink. She knows I rock at Trivial Pursuit. "What about Monopoly?"

"Good idea," Mum says, standing up. "The Wildgusts and Amy against the Sticklebacks." (Dan's name is Stickleback. Weird, I know, but there you go.)

"Sylvie," Dave warns. He obviously hasn't forgotten the last time Mum and Clover played Monopoly.

Clover loves to win and is totally unscrupulous. She steals houses and hotels and even money from the bank. It drives Mum insane. Last Christmas they had a huge row over it. Mum threw all the Monopoly money (she was the banker) in Clover's face.

"Take it all, Clover!" she screamed. "You may as well."

Clover just opened her mouth and tried to catch the fluttering notes between her teeth while Mum ran off in a steaming sulk. There's no way she'd be offering to play Monopoly with Clover—unless she intends to use Clover's tricks to her advantage.

"What?" Mum frowns at Dave. "You like Monopoly."

He keeps quiet. Wise.

"Right," Mum continues. "Can you help me find the box, Clover?"

From the looks Mum and Clover are exchanging, I know they're hatching something.

"I'll just check on the babies," I say, following closely behind them.

"Thanks, Amy." Dave raises his glass and smiles at me a little sloppily. I think he's had a bit too much wine.

I stand outside the living-room door. Mum and Clover are huddled in the far corner of the room, the Monopoly box open. A floorboard creaks under my foot, and they both look round guiltily.

"I'm just being the human baby monitor," I say. "Carry on with your espionage. Don't forget to put plenty of hotels up your sleeves."

"Amy," Clover hisses.

I smile at her knowingly and walk away.

"I don't care what you have to do," I hear Mum say as I go up the stairs. "We *must* win, understand?"

"Don't worry, sis," Clover says. "We'll trash them."

Jeepers! Mum's lost all her scruples. This feud with Prue must be serious.

Alex, Evie, Bella, and Ollie are sleeping soundly.

It takes me a few minutes to find Denis. He's sitting on his bed in the Lilac Room, carving the end of a large stick into a point with his penknife. I watch him for a second. He's using the blade like an expert, skimming the wood away from his body with firm, even strokes.

"Are you in the Scouts or something?" I ask him.

He jumps and his penknife clatters onto the floor. "So what if I am?" He glares at me, his dark eyes sparkling like coals in a fire. "You nearly made me wreck my spear." He waves the stick at me and prods me in the stomach.

"Ouch!" I jump back, rubbing my skin. "That hurt. Be careful."

He pokes me again.

"What are you doing? Stop or I'll—" I look closely at his face. There's a dark-brown ring around his mouth. "Have you been eating chocolate? I thought you weren't allowed sweets."

"No!" He rubs the back of his hand quickly across his lips.

"Look, if you brush your teeth and get into bed, I won't say anything, OK? Why don't you read a book?"

"Mum only packed Enid Blytons, and they're way too babyish."

"I saw some Anthony Horowitz books on the shelves in the living room. If I get one for you, will you go to bed?"

His eyes light up and he nods. "Don't tell Mum. She thinks they're too violent."

"Deal."

Violent? I think as I creep downstairs, feeling like a French Resistance spy. (The Nazis used to ban books too.) Denis has just attacked me with a stick. At least Alex Rider is polite to girls and tries to combat evil, not cause it. Denis might learn something.

I grab *Stormbreaker* off the bookshelf, run back upstairs, and thrust it into his eager hands. "If Prue finds it, cover for me."

He smiles. It lasts only a split second, but it's definitely a smile. Maybe I'm getting somewhere.

When I walk back into the kitchen, everyone looks up at me.

"What?" I say.

"You're playing with Dan and Prue," Clover says. "To even out the numbers."

"But what about Dave?" I ask. "He should play with his sister."

Mum glares at me, eyes flashing. "He's playing with us."

I glance around the table. You could almost eat the tension in the room. Everyone looks very serious. Especially Mum. Great, just my luck. But I know when to keep quiet, so I pull out a chair and sit down beside Dan.

Mum rubs her hands together and says, "Let the battle commence."

"I should warn you that I used to work for a real estate agent, Sylvie," Prue says. "I believe that gives our team a distinct advantage. Want to concede defeat while you still can?"

"Prue, you used to show houses on a Saturday," Dan says. "It's hardly relevant."

She glares at him. He murmurs, "Sorry," then stares down at the table.

I giggle nervously. No one else so much as grins.

Mum, Clover, and Dave win easily. Surprise, surprise.

Prue can't understand it. "But we own Shrewsbury Road, Ailesbury Road, *and* Grafton Street, the most expensive properties on the whole board." She's staring at the small cluster of little green houses in her hand and shaking her head.

"But they have so many hotels," Dan tells her gently. She's taking the loss very badly.

"I demand a rematch," she says, suddenly all feisty. She looks at Mum. "Trivial Pursuit." Mum opens her mouth to protest, but Prue doesn't let her speak. "I'm sure Amy will manage, won't you, Amy?"

I just nod. There's no way I'm getting involved in Mum and Prue's board-game mud wrestle.

"To make it fair," Prue adds, "Amy can answer the kids' questions. We brought Trivial Pursuit Junior for Denis."

I try not to laugh. I can't imagine Denis being interested in board games.

"We'll still win," Mum says.

"Let's see about that," Prue challenges her.

♥ Chapter 14

Wednesday lunchtime. It's bucketing down outside, and Mum still isn't talking to me. It's hardly my fault I'm so good at Trivial Pursuit. Mum said I didn't have to answer *all* the questions correctly; I could have gotten one or two wrong. But that goes against all my principles. I suppose I was showing off a bit, answering some of the adult pie questions as well as my own.

Clover tried to get me to help their team on the sly, but I was having none of it. They cheated their way through Monopoly; I was not going to let them win Trivial Pursuit too. Besides, I like Dan. He's funny. Yes, he can be a bit grumpy—but with Prue for a wife, who can blame him?

Mum's still holding it against me, though. She wouldn't let me drive into town with Clover to collect Brains, so I'm stuck inside, staring out at the gray drizzle. I'm all on my ownio. Mum and Dave have gone for a drive with the babies; Prue and Dan are doing educational arty-crafty things with Ollie and Bella in the living room. I've no idea where Denis is. Probably in a damp corner somewhere, stamping on snails.

But hang on a second: there's someone lurking in the shrubbery. Staring through the rain-splattered glass, I see that it's the gardener, Kit. I'm bored stiff, so I decide to brave talking to him. I wiggle my toes into my flip-flops and pull on a raincoat.

Before stepping outside, I try to calm my racing heart by taking deep breaths. I close my eyes and press my thumb and my first finger together, hoping to channel some inner calm.

"You look mental."

I peel my eyes open. Denis is standing in front of me. (His tummy is straining at the waist of his khaki shorts; it doesn't look very comfortable.)

"Takes one to know one," I retort. Not very original, I know, but I'm under pressure. "Now, run along, Denis. Go and find some slugs to torture."

"I prefer babies. Slugs don't scream. I'm gonna

gouge Bella's eyes out with my spear." He sniffs loudly before sticking a finger up his nose and twisting. Pulling it out again, he studies the tip, then wipes it on his shorts.

"Nice," I say. "I'm going for a walk. See you later."

Luckily, he doesn't follow me. As I look around the garden for Kit, I do feel a wee bit guilty. But Seth's in Italy. (Probably winking at Tinker Bell.) And Kit's right here, in the rain somewhere. I gulp nervously and try to remember Clover's advice on getting a boy to notice you. "Be yourself," I mumble as I search the flower beds. "Smile. Listen. Be natural. Show an interest in his hobbies."

I stop. Hobbies? Did we really say that? *Hobbity hobbies?*

I wonder if Clover has filed the problem page yet. Hobbies sounds so lame, so 1980s Girl Guide badges. Knitting is a hobby; if you're Denis, carving sticks with a penknife is a hobby; building model yachts is a hobby. (Boys — are boys a hobby?) Music, rugby, clothes, hockey, they're not hobbies. They're a part of who you are. Interests, that sounds better. (Boys are definitely an interest.)

And as my mind is clicking away, planning how to edit the agony aunt reply and make it better, there he is, right in front of me — Kit. Forking grass clippings into one of the compost bins. He's wearing an enormous yellow fisherman's raincoat, laced at the neck. Underneath, I can just see the bottom of a pair of white-and-navy Hawaiian board shorts. Streams of water are running down his bare, muscular calves, and he has black Reefs on his tanned feet. I stare at his silver toe ring and the inky black Celtic tattoo around his ankle.

"Nice day," he says with a grin. Even drenched and wearing that old raincoat, he still looks edible.

I drag my eyes upward and meet his. *Zing!* Oh, dear God, he's even better-looking close up, if that's possible. I nod mutely, my heart thumping loudly.

He rests his pitchfork on the grass, prongs upward, like a devil's, and stares at me. "Hate fruit flies." He eyes the top of the open compost bin. "Not so many in the rain."

I nod again. *Say something, Amy.* He's going to think you're some kind of mute weirdo. "I'm Amy," I manage. "I'm staying in Haven House with my family." It comes out as a squeak.

"Aye," he says. "I know that."

"And you're Kit. Martie told me."

"Did she, now?" His eyes narrow, probably

because he's wondering what else she said, but he still doesn't speak. Instead, he goes back to staring at the compost bin.

Talk about awkward conversations: water from a stone and all that. But I'm not going to give up yet. "Um, we have compost bins at home," I say, then wince. *Brilliant, Amy. Inspired.* Not! But he looks at me and seems interested, so I carry on. "And a wormery. We use the compost for Mum's roses."

He still says nothing. (He's clearly blown away by my scintillating conversational skills. As if.)

"They're my favorite flowers," I add, then stop. I've completely run out of things to say.

"There's a rose garden here," he says after an agonizingly long silence.

"Really? Cool. I love the way roses smell. I like white ones the best. And pink and red. But white mostly. Have you ever seen a blue one? They're quite unusual, but I have—" I clamp my mouth shut before I can spout any more rubbish. I stand there feeling useless while he forks the last bits of grass into the compost bin and slams it shut.

"Follow me, so," he says.

"Where's your dog?" I ask as he throws the fork into the rusty old wheelbarrow.

"Jack? Sheltering. Doesn't like rain. Sensible lad."

He leads the way around the high granite wall to the side wing of the house, where there is another narrow gateway.

"Door to the rose garden," he says. He pulls a jangling set of keys out of his pocket, searches for one, then unlocks the padlock. He grinds back the rusty bolt and stands aside to let me walk in first.

I half expect him to push me from behind and ram the bolt home, trapping me forever in a creepy dungeon full of bats and flesh-eating rats — but clearly I've been watching too many horror movies with Clover. He's just being polite — which instantly reminds me of Seth. Seth's manners are fairy-tale good. Polly has terrorized him into it.

Seth.

I feel a twist of guilt in my stomach. But as I walk through the gate, I forget everything; I'm so overwhelmed by the remarkable smell. It's like walking into Clover's bedroom after she's just sprayed herself with her posh perfume. Only better. Because this scent is the real thing. I take long, heady breaths and start to walk down the wet cobblestone path; the rounded stones press into the soles of my flip-flops, giving my feet a pebble massage.

I look around me. I'm in a tiny walled garden, full of waist-high rose bushes. The beds have been separated into four quadrants, each one full of white, red, light-pink, or dark-pink roses, each smelling subtly different. In the middle is a paved circle with a fountain: a stone dolphin with a trickle of water splashing out of its mouth. I walk toward it and study the water in its mossy pool, expecting to see goldfish or a magical frog, but it's full of murky water and dark-green weeds.

"It's beautiful — like *The Secret Garden*." I beam at him. (I can't help it; it's just so unexpected.) "Thank you so much for showing me this place. The smell" — I give a big sniff — "it's just amazing. . . ."

Kit smiles. "No bother. There's something else I want to show you." He beckons me and leads the way past the fountain.

Hidden behind a carpet of climbing roses is an open-fronted shed. Well, not a shed exactly, more of a summerhouse — freshly painted eggshell blue — with latticework on its three walls and a conical turreted roof. There's a little seat in it.

"This was Mam's favorite place," Kit says. "Used to sit here and sniff, just like you did. Said the roses smelled like heaven in the rain. She were a chatterbox too."

I laugh. "Used to?"

"She's dead," he says simply.

"How terrible—what happened?" The question's out before I can stop it.

"Drowned in the lough."

I gasp.

Something flickers across his face, but he recovers quickly and says, "It were an accident. A boating accident."

"I'm so sorry," I murmur, not knowing what else to say.

"'S OK. Ancient history now. Haven't been in the water since, though. Don't like boats, neither."

"But it's an island. How do you get here in the mornings?"

"I live here, in the old boathouse. Esther doesn't mind. Martie brings me shopping most days. And if I need to reach the mainland, I can. At low tide you can walk to the shore on the far side of the island. Over the rocks. But don't try it; it's dangerous." He looks awkward again; his eyes shift toward the ground, and he rubs a bit of moss away from the path with the toe of his Reef. "Best get back to work," he adds.

As I follow him out of the garden, I wonder absently if the lovely Kit has a girlfriend to talk to, someone special. What a waste if he doesn't. There's something so attractive about his quiet, self-contained manner. He's solid and earthy; almost rooted to the ground. Maybe if he doesn't . . . No, Amy. *Stop*, I tell myself. Think of Seth.

You'd think I'd be happy with one boyfriend. But it just goes to show, we're never really happy with what we've got, are we?

♥ Chapter 15

I'm sitting on my zebra-print duvet in the Room That Taste Forgot, feeling a bit sad and down. I've been trying to write Seth a letter, but I can't concentrate. I run my finger along the exotic feathers hanging from the edge of the bedside lampshade and then study one of the scary black-and-red wooden African masks on the wall. Suddenly, Denis smashes through the door with his shoulder, slamming the metal handle against the wall.

"Hey!" I shriek. "I could have been changing. Knock, Shrek-Face!"

He ignores me. "Brains is here. Clover told me to tell you."

"What's that?" I point at the white plastic bag he's clutching in his sweaty hands.

He holds it against his chest. "Mine," he snaps, like Gollum in *The Lord of the Rings*.

I roll my eyes at him. "You'd better not have stolen anything." Jumping down off the bed, I push Denis out of the room (no joke, I can tell you) before walking out myself and closing the door firmly behind me. "Barge in again without knocking and I'll tell your mum about the Horror-witz book. *Comprende?*"

He pokes his tongue out at me and strolls off toward his own room.

"How's my favorite hot potato?" Brains is walking up the stairs, a black kit bag slung over his shoulder. His coconut-brown Afro is held back off his face with a thin scarlet hair elastic, and he's wearing a banana-yellow T-shirt, billowing white silk shorts, and gold Converse high-tops. Ah, yes, the legendary Brains "style."

"Hey, Brains." I grin at him. "How was your trip?"

"Groovy. 'Cause I've got a ticket to ride." He bursts into an old Beatles song and starts waggling his head, making it go all floppy, like a string puppet, and shaking his shoulders.

"He's got Beatlemania," Clover explains. "The

Golden Lions have a wedding gig next week. They've been given a playlist. Loads of old stuff."

"Oldies but goldies," Brains says. "Big spondu-licks too. We can cut a demo on the proceeds, so don't knock it, buttercup." He breaks into another, even odder, song, with the lyrics "Build me up, Buttercup."

I giggle. "What on earth is that?"

Clover shakes her head. "Awful, isn't it? Don't encourage him." She points into the Lilac Room. "Brains, you're in there."

He sticks his head through the door. "Me on my lonesome tonight?"

"Yep. And no Elvis songs, please."

He dumps his bag on the floor and jumps onto one of the double beds. "Pretty comfy, Clover," he says, wiggling his eyebrows and giving her a sugges-tive wink.

"Uh-uh." She shakes her head, laughing. "Brains, while we're under the same roof as my sis and Prue, my Amish aunt, I don't think so."

"Not even a liddle-iddle cuddle?"

"No! So don't go getting any ideas."

"Prue doesn't approve." He chuckles. "Hey, there's a song in that." He fists a hand in front of his mouth as if he's clutching a microphone. "Wanna kiss my babe," he sings in a husky rock voice. "But that Prudie Prue doesn't approve. Gotta no groove. Doesn't approve—" He stops suddenly and stares at the doorway.

You guessed it. Prue is leaning against the door frame, her lips pressed together like two thin pink worms. She does not look impressed. Oops.

"Who gave Denis the sweets?" she demands, holding up a familiar-looking, now-empty plastic bag.

Clover gives a little cough. She opens her mouth to say something, but Brains is too quick for her.

"*Moi*," he says. "*Je suis* guilty. Arrival present."

You'd hardly think it possible, but Prue's lips go even thinner. "Denis is not allowed sugar. He's on a diet. You may have noticed that he's not exactly thin."

Brains shrugs. "Hey, don't sweat the small stuff. I was pudgy until my teens. Then I went Svelte City." He waves a hand down his slim body.

"You were fat?" a little voice from behind Prue pipes up. It's Denis.

"I sure was, little buddy. Fat as Fats Domino."

Prue looks flabbergasted. "Denis isn't fat; he just has big bones."

Brains smiles at her. "Never said he was, ma'am. But me, I was *fat*."

"None of this is very constructive," Prue says, flustered. "Go back to your room, Denis."

"This is my room," he says.

"That was only until . . . um . . . Brains . . . arrived," Prue says, stumbling over Brains's name. "You're in with Ollie now—you know that. And no arguments, please."

Denis mumbles something, but Prue glares him into submission. "OK, OK, I'm going," he mutters, heading off down the corridor.

"Hey, the little dude can camp in here with me," Brains says. "Plenty of room for a nipper. I don't mind."

Denis turns back, his face brightening a little.

Prue blinks a few times. She's clearly never met anyone quite like Brains before. Maybe she doesn't understand what he's just said.

"Brains is offering to share the room with Denis," I say, trying to be helpful.

"I have ears," Prue practically spits. "I heard what he said! But I don't think it's a very good idea. It might give Denis . . . *notions*."

Denis scowls at his mum's back and then runs off, just as Dan appears behind her.

Dan puts his head on Prue's shoulder. She winces but doesn't shrug him away.

"There you are," he says to her.

"Hey, Dan," Clover says. "Brains said Denis can bunk in here with him. Might be more fun for him than sharing with Ollie. What do you think?"

Dan looks at Brains. "Are you sure? He can be quite a handful."

"*No problemo*," Brains says. "I'm used to kids. Have a little sis at home."

"I don't think it's such a good idea," Prue says. "Denis is a restless sleeper."

Brains shrugs. "I sleep like a log; won't bother me one iota."

Dan smiles. "And you can always send him outside if he's farting too much."

"Dan!" Prue looks horrified. "Please."

"It might be exactly what Denis needs. A bit of boy time. Go on, Prue."

"Why don't you have a trial run?" I suggest. "If Denis behaves himself tonight, he gets to stay with Brains. If he doesn't, then banish him to Ollie's room."

"You always were the smart one, Beanie," Clover says, ruffling my hair.

Prue can hardly refuse now without looking petty, so she glares at me instead. Double oops. Then behind her back I spot Denis peeping around the corner. He catches my eye. I smile at him, and he smiles back for a second before pulling his face into a scowl. Two scowling Sticklebacks and a partridge in a pear tree. Lucky old me!

♥ Chapter 16

Later that evening the parentals are watching an ancient film called *The Big Chill*; Brains says the soundtrack is hopping—Motown and the Rolling Stones—so he's watching it too.

Clover and I are holed up in the Lilac Room. Brains has set up his Wii on the portable telly, and Clover's thrashing her opponent in the boxing ring. Gramps is reading in his room, the littlies are all in bed, and I have no idea where Denis is lurking.

"Thump." Clover hits the air with the Wii controller. *"Thump, thump, thump. Bash."*

"You're pretty good at that," I say, watching her annihilate the other boxer.

"Brains is obsessed. Plays it all the time. What is it with boys and computer games?"

I shrug. "Not all boys. Seth's not a huge fan."

She pauses the match. "How is lover boy getting on in Roma?"

"Fine, I think. He sent me an e-mail today, but it was a bit funny."

"Funny ha-ha or funny peculiar?"

"Funny peculiar."

"Why?"

I shrug again. "Don't know. Maybe he's going off me."

"Did you print it out?"

"Yes, why?"

"Read it to me while I sock it to this sucker. I'll translate for you. Boy talk can be rather cryptic." She starts punching again.

I'm glad Clover hasn't asked to read the e-mail herself—I've scribbled all over it and each time he mentioned Jin, I numbered it. I know I'm probably reading too much into it, but sometimes I just can't help myself.

Dear Amy, *What happened to "Hey, babe"???*

How's tricks? It's v. hot here. Polly's even getting a tan through her clothes—I thought she was joking until she showed me the freckles on her arm. Jin⁽¹⁾ says Polly should wear denser tops; linen has a very loose weave. Jin⁽²⁾ wants to study fashion in college, so she should know.

"Jin's this girl in the arty-farty commune," I explain to Clover. "She's seventeen and wears bikini tops every day."

"Hmm," Clover says, and bites the inside of her lip. "Keep reading."

Polly's course is going well. She says one of the men has real talent, but the rest of them are just dabblers. She's been busing them all over the place so they can take photos of crooked trees and run-down farm buildings.

Yesterday Polly dragged me and Jin⁽³⁾ to Saint Peter's Cathedral. *Why exactly did Jin rummy tag along???*

They almost didn't let Jin⁽⁴⁾ inside 'cause of her bikini top.   *Not the bloody bikini top again!*

But Polly had a T-shirt on under her shirt, so she gave it to Jin.⁽⁵⁾ Jin⁽⁶⁾ said it smelled of perfume.

She must stink! Jin⁽⁷⁾ doesn't use any artificial products on her hair or her body — she says they pollute your system and give you cancer.

The best bit about the trip was climbing up to the dome and looking down. Jin[8] hates heights, so it was just me and Polly. Polly took some mega pics. Jin[9] was way impressed.

"OK, enough already!" Clover pauses the game again and puts her hands in the air. "Why does he keep going on about this Jin girl? Is he trying to make you jealous or what?"

"Maybe he just likes her more than me."

Clover frowns, her face creasing up like a pug dog's. "No way. She's a serial bikini abuser; she's clearly riddled with low self-esteem."

"Or oodles of it," I suggest. "Her boobs probably wobble when she walks. Boys like girls who wobble."

"Oh, Beanie." Clover sighs. "I hate to say it, but you're right. Boys are pretty sad. Even Brains ogles girls with jelly puppies."

I scrunch up my nose. "Puppies?"

"Boobs. Blame Brains; it's his word."

"So what can I do about Jin?"

"While he's away, nothing, I'm afraid. Just act normal. Don't let him know the whole Jin-a-ding thing is getting to you."

"I could tell him about Kit."

"Kit? You mean the gardener?"

I nod.

Clover smirks and raises her eyebrows.

"I don't like him or anything," I protest. "Just to make Seth jealous."

She shrugs. "You could. But you're bigger than that. Don't stoop to his level. Stay aloof. It might be just a fleeting crush. If Brains was here, he'd start singing 'Puppy Love.'"

I start to smile, but it turns into a sigh. "I hope you're right." I don't tell Clover about the Xs. Today Seth only gave me three Xs. Three! In his letter, he gave me three *rows*. I'm utterly depressed.

"Can I play?"

I've been moping on the lilac bed for half an hour, watching Clover play on the Wii, when I hear Denis's shrill voice.

"Can I play?" he asks again.

"No. Go away, Spawn," I mutter. I'm in no mood for him.

"Poor Amy-damy's got the boyfriend blues," Clover tells him. "I wouldn't go too close to her; she might bite."

"Amy's got a boyfriend," Denis chants. "Amy's got a boyfriend."

"Don't tell Mum," Denis says. I've washed the gunge from around his mouth and made him drink a glass of water.

He's lying in bed now, the lilac duvet pulled up to his chin. A plump tear runs down his cheek and lands on the pillow. I start to feel sorry for him. He's a big mess.

He admitted to sneaking downstairs to steal a whole bag of mini Kit Kats, a giant bag of tortilla chips, half a loaf of white bread, and a large box of Coco Pops from the kitchen. He ate it all, except for a third of the box of Coco Pops, and then hid the evidence under Brains's bed.

"Why did you eat all that food?" I ask, sitting on the bed. I want to wipe away his tears, but something stops me. "No wonder you were sick."

His lips turn down and his chin starts to wobble.

"Denis, talk to me."

"But you hate me," he sobs. "Everyone hates me. Even my mum and dad hate me."

I'm shocked. He sounds so unhappy.

"No, they don't," I say. "They may not like what you do sometimes, but I'm pretty sure they love you."

He snorts. "They fight about me all the time. They

think I can't hear them, but I can. They're always going on about my weight and stuff. I'm worried they'll get a divorce, and it'll be all my fault."

My stomach flips. My parents used argue all the time too and think that I couldn't hear them. They'd close the kitchen door tight and then start taking verbal lumps out of each other. And I could hear everything. Everything. The same accusations, over and over.

Tears prick my eyes. Poor Denis. No kid should have to listen to their parents arguing.

"All parents fight sometimes," I say gently. "It doesn't mean they're going to get a divorce — they seem pretty solid to me. And they talk about you because they love you and are trying to help you."

Denis burps.

I watch him for a moment, hoping he won't get sick again. "You OK?" I ask.

He nods. "Just feel a bit funny."

"That's normal after getting sick. And, Denis, if you keep on binge eating like that, you'll get even bigger."

He presses his lips together, just like Prue.

"I'm sorry, Denis, but it's the truth."

He's silent for a bit, then says, "Don't tell Mum about me getting sick. Promise?"

I think about this. He must be pretty miserable to shove all that food into himself. Dry white bread isn't even that tasty. I know Prue would have a fit if I told her what he's been up to, and Denis would probably never speak to me again. Strange though it may sound, I want him to feel he can talk to *someone*.

"OK, I promise," I say. "But you have to stop eating so much. Eat more at dinner if you're hungry." Great, now I sound like my mother.

I obviously sound like Prue, too, because he clamps one hand over his eyes and rocks from side to side. "Go 'way. Go 'way. Go 'way."

"I'm only trying to help."

He lashes out at me with his other arm, and I jump backward, frightened. "OK, OK, I'm going."

Jeez, he's one mixed-up kid.

♥ Chapter 17

Clover drives Gramps to his date with Esther on Thursday evening. Brains and I are tagging along for the ride — and to spy on Gramps, of course. It's not often you get to check out a sixty-five-year-old on a date.

"You guys OK back there?" Clover asks us. Gramps is in the front, and Brains and I are squashed into the back of her Mini Cooper, like hippos in airplane seats. I'm surviving, but Brains's long legs are rammed against the back of Clover's seat.

"Comfy is as comfy does," Brains says.

I grin. I have no idea what he's talking about half the time, but he makes me laugh so much it doesn't really matter.

"Do you think she'll like the chocolates?" Gramps asks. He's gripping a scarlet box with a gold bow in his shaking hands. He keeps flipping the sun visor down and looking at his teeth in the small rectangular mirror.

"She'll love them," Clover assures him.

Gramps goes silent and stares out the window, probably lost in thought about his first love, Esther. But hang on: he's not staring out the window at all, he's blowing on it and sniffing the air.

"Gramps, your breath is fine," Clover says. "Quit worrying. It's not as if you're going to be . . . Wait a sec, you're not going to snog Esther in front of us, are you? You'll damage Amy forever! And what if your false teeth get locked together?"

"I don't have false teeth!" Gramps snorts indignantly. "And we're not going to *snog*, Clover. Please! And watch your language around Esther. She's a lady."

"*Snog* isn't a bad word, Gramps," I say. "It just means kiss. With tongues."

"Amy Green!" Gramps sounds shocked. "What do you know about kissing with tongues?"

Clover giggles and I just stare down at my hands. Oops.

"Don't answer that," Gramps says. "In my day, thirteen-year-olds —"

"Walked to school in bare feet through the snow and ate coal," Clover says, her voice warbling as though she's ancient. "Them were the bad ol' days all right. No electricity, donkeys instead of cars, and no telly."

"No telly?" Brains pipes up. "Were you very poor, Mr. Wildgust?"

Gramps laughs. "Len, please. No one had a telly when I was growing up, Brains. They only started selling them in the 1950s, and they cost the same amount as a small car. Mona and I got our first black-and-white set in the early seventies, when Sylvie was little. She used to love *Flower Pot Men* and *Larry the Lamb*. Simple days."

"Somebody stop him," Clover quips, "or he'll start waxing lyrical about the day he met the Beatles."

"You met the Beatles?" Brains is all ears. "No way, man."

Clover shakes her head discouragingly, but it's too late — Gramps is in his stride.

"Oh, I did, Brains, I did. It was back in 1963 at the Gresham Hotel. The Beatles were visiting Dublin to appear on *The Showband Show,* and I was working at RTÉ at the time as a broadcast assistant."

I zone out. I've heard the story so many times I could parrot it. "Met" is a bit of an exaggeration, although he did exchange a few words with Ringo Starr, the drummer, about the rubbish Irish weather while he was adjusting his microphone.

Seth likes the Beatles too. I miss him so much. Neither of our mobiles roams abroad, and it feels unnatural, being cut off from him like this. I keep thinking of things I want to tell him and can't. By the time I get around to sitting down to e-mail him, the moment has passed or I've forgotten what I wanted to say. And I still haven't written him that letter.

I wonder what he's up to right now. Not stuck in a car with two deranged music fans gibbering on like monkeys, that's for sure.

When we arrive at Esther's house, Martie is just getting into her car. She looks a little worried. "Ah, the Dublin gang," she says, walking over to us, Dante at her heels. "Don't suppose you know any good bands? I'm at my wits' end." She runs her hands through her short hair, making it stick up like the top of a pineapple. "I urgently need one for Saturday night. Ours has double booked." She shakes her head. "It was supposed to be the highlight of regatta week."

Clover and I both look at Brains.

He's way ahead of us. "The Golden Lions, at your service"—he grins, puts his hand on his chest, and bows grandly—"playing whatever your heart desires. From the Beatles to U2 and back again." He breaks into the chorus of U2's "I Still Haven't Found What I'm Looking For," complete with Elvis hip wiggles and a couple of "Hey, baby's" thrown in for good measure.

From the expression on her face, I think Martie's more shocked than impressed.

"They're very good," Clover reassures her. "They really get the crowd going."

"And are you available on Saturday night?" Martie asks Brains.

"For you, purdy lady, I sure am." He winks and doffs an imaginary hat.

Martie smiles. "In that case, crisis over. I think we've found our band." She takes Brains's details and saves them into her mobile, then turns to Gramps and winks. "Enjoy your date, Mr. Wildgust. Esther is all ready for you." She looks around at the rest of us. "Are you all going?"

"Nah," Clover says, "we're just Gramps's chauffeurs. We'll be back for lover boy later."

* * *

Clover lied. She's determined to stick around and spy on Gramps, so after leaving him outside Esther's house, she drives down the rickety road and parks the car in the entrance to a field. Brains says he'll stay put and ring the other Golden Lions. "Invasion of the old dude's privacy. And I need to sort out this jiggy-jig gig."

"You just want a nap, don't you?" Clover laughs. "You're the Mayor of Lazytown."

Brains puts his seat back and settles into it, purring like a cat.

We walk back to Esther's. Her cottage looks ancient, with its mottled whitewashed walls, old-fashioned wooden Dutch door, and garden path made of dark slate set into the mossy grass. There's a fast-flowing river at the back of the house, and a tire hangs from a nearby tree, dangling over the water. It must be fun to swing on it and drop into the swirling river below.

We creep around the house, looking in the small, high windows. Nothing. Then we see a greenhouse running along the back wall. And inside, sitting at a round metal table, a string of white fairy lights above them, are Gramps and Esther, looking pretty cozy.

We press our backs against the wall, but they haven't spotted us. They're too busy laughing and smiling at each other.

"Looks like it's going well," Clover says in a low voice, her eyes fixed on the happy couple.

I nod as Gramps takes Esther's hand and gives it a kiss. Yuck!

"Let's go," I whisper. I don't feel comfortable spying on them.

Just then Esther says something and Gramps stands up. He reaches up to the fairy lights, then hollers, "Ow!" and whips his hand away.

I jump, Clover squeals, and we both run back around the house and down the lane.

"Why did you scream?" I ask her breathlessly when we stop at the car.

"You stood on my foot." She reaches down and squeezes her toes. They do look a bit red.

"Well, if you must wear flip-flops on James Bond missions . . ."

Brains zips down the window. "What's up, Jelly Bean?" he asks me. "The golden oldies snogging yet?"

"No. I think Gramps got stung or something. Then we ran away."

He chuckles. "You'd never cut it as Charlie's Angels, girls. Let's vamoose."

* * *

Ten minutes later, Clover's mobile rings.

It's Gramps.

"You have to rescue me," he hisses wildly over the speakerphone. "I've locked myself in the loo, and I daren't come out. Esther's crazier than crazy golf. She's trying to kill me!"

♥ Chapter 18

As we drive up the lane, Esther's dogs growl and bark at us. They're German shepherds and the size of small horses. We beep three times, and Gramps rushes out of the house. His face is clown red, and there are big muddy paw prints on his best cream cords.

Esther appears, smirking in the doorway, and folds her arms across her chest. "And don't come back!" she yells as he clambers into the car.

"You OK, Gramps?" Clover asks.

"Just drive. Quick!" he says frantically. One of the German shepherds leaps up at his window, barking and smearing the glass with its paws. Gramps jumps in his seat. "Get me away from this place!"

As Clover powers down the bumpy drive, Gramps begins to fill us in on what happened. "As soon as I walked in the door, Esther lurched against me and spilled elderberry wine all down the front of my trousers." He winces. "I looked like I'd wet myself. And it gets worse. I went into the greenhouse, where we were eating, and there was a dead rat on my chair. It was just sitting there, staring at me!"

Brains and I make gagging noises.

Clover says, "You're a pair of big girl's blouses. Rats can't hurt you when they're dead. Continue, Gramps."

"It gets far worse," he says. "Next, I got electrocuted."

"What?" I ask.

"Man, this is getting so weird," Brains adds.

"It's true!" Gramps says. "The fairy lights weren't working and Esther asked me to try and fix them, but as soon as I touched the wire . . . *POW!* I thought my arm was going to fall off! It went all numb and then all tingly. She was lucky she didn't give me a heart attack."

"Surely, she apologized," Clover says.

Gramps shakes his head. "No, she just muttered something about finally getting what I deserved. I'm telling you, she's completely barking mad."

"Why didn't you just leave, Gramps?" I ask.

"I thought about it, but I was hungry, and Esther always was a great little cook."

Clover laughs. "So you decided to brave it out until you'd been fed."

"Well, yes. Terrible idea. She dumped my steak in my lap! Just like that. And then her blooming dogs started to attack me, trying to get at the meat. It was terrifying! And all Esther did was throw back her head and cackle like a witch. 'That'll teach you, Len Wildgust,' she said. 'You won't forget me *now*, will you!'"

"Maybe she *was* trying to kill you," Clover murmurs.

Gramps gives a loud harrumph. "'Course she was; that's what I've been trying to tell you. Well, I'd had enough then, so I ran into the hall, locked myself in the loo, and rang you."

"And we saved you." Clover grins. "I do like a good rescue."

I sit back in my seat. When it comes to odd behavior, it just goes to show, age means *nada*. You'd have thought Esther would have forgotten all about being stood up—but oh, no, even after forty years she's still bearing a grudge the size of a small continent. But you have to hand it to her: for an old lady, she's full of new tricks.

When we get back to Haven House, Gramps goes straight upstairs to change his trousers. "Not a word to Sylvie about any of this, understand?" he says firmly. "Or to any of the others."

"What's it worth?" Clover says.

He just glares at her and storms off.

Brains and Clover go upstairs to work on the Golden Lions' playlist for regatta night. At least, that's what they say they're up to, but I think they just want some time alone. They haven't snogged all day. Brains kept swatting Clover away and nodding in my direction. He's too sweet. But judging by the way she grabbed his arm and frog-marched him up the stairs, I'd say she's having kissing withdrawal symptoms.

I walk into the kitchen and catch Prue swigging out of a wine bottle. *Prue!* I nearly faint. I give a cough and she swings around, spitting red wine all down her white top.

"For heaven's sake, Amy," she says. "Why are you sneaking around like that? You gave me a start."

I stare at her. She's wearing a pair of cutoff denim shorts that barely cover her bum, a camisole with spaghetti straps, and white wedge sandals. She's not wearing a bra, and her large breasts are pressing against the cotton, firm and perky like Barbie's. I'm impressed. Why does she hide them under those prim shirts all the time?

She hiccups.

"Are you OK, Prue?"

"Never better," she says, lurching to the left and steadying herself on the kitchen counter. "What are you up to, Amy?" She hiccups again. Her breath smells fruity, and her tongue is blood red.

"Just getting a Coke. See ya." I leave her to it and walk into the pantry to grab a can. I hear someone walk into the kitchen.

"There you are, Prue." It's Dan. "Are you coming back inside?" he goes on. "We're just about to start Scrabble."

"Scrabble?" Prue laughs a little manically. "Scrabble?! Can't we do something more exciting? How about strip poker? Or spin the bottle? Do you think Dave would be up for it? I'd say it's right up Sylvie's street."

Is this really Prue? Intrigued, I spy on them through the crack between the pantry door and the wall.

"Prue!" Dan says, sounding shocked. He pulls the wine bottle rather roughly out of her hand. "Haven't you had enough? Why don't you take a nice nap? Or go for a walk." He cups a hand under her elbow and tries to steer her out of the kitchen.

Prue is having none of it; staggering a little, she pulls her elbow out of his hand. "Don't want a walk. Want to have fun. Why don't we have fun anymore, Big Bear?" She snuggles up to him. "Let's go skinny-dipping, just the two of us. It'd be romantic." She gives a fruity burp.

I press my hand over my mouth and try not to laugh.

"It's cold outside, Prue," Dan says, struggling to hold her up.

"Not that cold!" she squeals, peeling off her top.

I screw my eyes tightly closed. But it's too late; I've already seen her boobs. What an eyeful! That's what you get for spying.

♥ Chapter 19

We arrive at Mary Ann's bar in Castletownshend just after eight on Saturday night.

It's a warm evening and people are spilling out onto the street, standing under the fluttering bunting, chatting and laughing.

Prue and Dan kindly offered to stay at home to mind Evie and Alex with their own brood. After the other night, Dan's probably afraid to let Prue near alcohol. She was back to her ironed jeans and buttoned-up shirt uniform on Friday morning and has been in a very grumpy mood ever since. Everyone has steered well clear of her.

Gramps stayed put too. I think he's still traumatized by his near-death experience with Esther.

Clover's wearing a tiny gold-sequined mini over white three-quarter-length leggings, gold flip-flops, a white cotton tank top with a golden sun embroidered on the front, and a gold-sequined head scarf tied in a knot under her chin, like a disco Queen Mum.

Even in my new black-and-white stripy T-shirt, white jeans, silver belt, and ballet pumps, I feel a bit dowdy beside her. I've even clipped two silver butterfly hair clips in my hair and layered more glittery green Urban Decay eye shadow onto my eyelids, but I still don't look as good as Clover.

Inside, the pub's rammed with bods. We have to wiggle our way through the sweaty hordes to find Brains. We eventually spot him with his band in the beer garden, setting up their equipment.

Clover whistles under her breath and pokes me in the side to get my attention. "Would you look at Dr. McSteamy over there?"

"Which one?" I stare over at the band.

"*Him*. Hubba-hubba. Must be the new lead guitar." Clover is staring at a tall, muscular boy with a tattoo of a skull on his hand. He's adjusting the strings of his guitar. "I do like a tasty indie boy. Hubba-hubba," she says again. "He can tighten my strings any time." She gives a dirty laugh.

"Clover! Brains is just over there, remember?"

At the sound of his name, Brains lifts his head. "Hey — it's our very own teenage fan club." He grins and waves us over.

The boy with the skull tattoo looks up, presses his lips together in an impressive bee-stung pout, and cocks his head. "You must be Clover." He checks her out. "And *you* must be Amy. Brains has told me all about you both." His eyes lock on mine. "Are you really only thirteen? You look older."

"Thanks." I grin like an idiot and he gives me a slow wink. My stomach flips. Clover's right. He is something. Green eyes, long dark Bambi eyelashes — totally wasted on a boy — white scar on his top lip.

"I'm Felix," he says. "Lead guitar. Fender Stratocaster, to be precise." He strokes his guitar with pride. "Isn't she a beauty?"

"And here's the man with the plan. Diablo," Brains says. A wiry, freckled guy smiles from under a shaggy strawberry-blond fringe.

"Hiya, girls," he says chirpily. "Nice to see you again, Clover. How are the ol' hols treating you? Weather OK? Been swimming yet? Any jellyfish in the water?" He says all this without waiting for an answer, shooting his words out like gunfire, *rat-a-tat-tat*.

He's about to open his mouth again when Barra the drummer says, "Lions, are we ready to roar?" He rubs his drumsticks together.

"Sure thing," Felix says easily.

Brains nods. "Bring it on. Bang a gong. Riff out the intro, Diablo, my man."

We move away as Diablo starts to play the opening bars of "A Little Less Conversation" (an old Elvis song) on his keyboard. A crowd begins to gather, and Brains grabs the microphone. There are cheers and claps as he belts out the first line in his strong, clear voice.

"Hey, they rock!" Martie says, appearing beside us. "What a relief." She's wearing black shorts and a silver-sequined T-shirt. There's a trace of mascara on her lashes, and her lips are a glossy pink. Her outfit is simple, yet stunning.

"Last year's band," she continues loudly over the music. "One word: brutal. Two old geezers with blue satin shirts and false teeth, singing along to backing tracks. These lads are cool. And would you at look him. . . ." She fans herself with her hand as Felix goes down on one knee for a guitar solo. "A star in the making if ever I saw one."

"I can introduce you later if you like," Clover offers.

"Nah. Thanks — but I don't do stars. Never know where you are with them."

"Diablo's nice. Not at all starry."

Martie smiles. "Thanks, Clover, but I'm off men for Lent."

Clover grins. "Oh, I've been there, girlfriend. *Muchos, muchos* times. But a girl can always look." She gazes at Felix again.

I spot Mum to the left of the crowd, also gazing adoringly at Felix. I shake my head. Cringe City. Mum's so embarrassing.

By ten o'clock, the Golden Lions are in full swing, tearing through the Beatles' back catalog, from "Yellow Submarine" to "Love Me Do."

"And here's something a little different, especially for Clover," Brains says. "'Mamma Mia.'"

"Yeah!" Clover claps her hands together and starts wiggling her hips. She grabs Mum's hand and makes her dance too. "Up on the table, Sylvie," she yells at her.

I find it hard to believe, but apparently Mum was a big table dancer once upon a time. Clover swears there's video footage somewhere of Mum prancing around on a table at her and Dad's wedding. I've never seen it, but I'm taking Clover's word for it.

Dave frowns. "That table doesn't look all that steady."

"Don't be such an old man," Mum says. "We're very light. It'll be fine." She climbs up, followed by Clover and then Martie. They all throw their arms in the air and bump hips to the music.

"Why don't you join them?" Dave asks me.

I shake my head. To be honest, I'm a bit self-conscious about dancing. And I'm certainly not going to draw any extra attention to my lack of coordination by dancing on a table.

"You were great on the guitar," I say, changing the subject.

Earlier, Dave joined the Golden Lions for U2's "One" and "With or Without You." He played Brains's acoustic guitar. I thought he'd look like a dinosaur beside Brains and the boys, but he was so confident and natural on the stage that I was blown away. For a second I forgot he was my almost stepdad.

"Thanks. I miss performing, Amy. But, hey, life goes on." He shrugs. "But there's something I've been meaning to talk to —" And I get the feeling he's about to launch into some sort of confession, when *CRACK!* The table collapses, and bottles and bodies tumble out of the sky and crash down to earth.

OK, that's a bit of an exaggeration. Basically, the

Golden Lions stop playing, there are a lot of shrieks and screams, two beer bottles smash on the stone paving — and Mum and Clover slide down the table on top of Martie.

"Girl sandwich!" Clover shouts. "Everyone OK? Sylvie? Martie?"

Mum gets up and brushes herself down, nodding, and Martie is laughing so much she can't speak.

"Guess that's a yes," Clover says. "How about 'Dancing Queen,' Brains?" she calls over to him.

He gives her a thumbs-up and launches into the song.

Clover grabs my hand. "Come on, Beanie. Shake a tail feather."

This time I do. And once I've stopped worrying about who's laughing at my horrible dancing, I start to really enjoy myself. I wave my arms in the air and sing along.

♥ Chapter 20

It's the day after the Golden Lions gig, and Mum and Prue are knocking lumps out of each other in the kitchen. Not literally, although from the dragon look in Mum's eyes earlier, it might not be all that long. The two of them have been itching for a fight all day.

Clover is listening in, her ear pressed against the gap between the wall and the kitchen door. She looks shocked. And believe me, it takes a lot to shock Clover.

"What are they arguing about this time? Fizzy drinks? Or eco-nappies versus Pampers? Yawn."

Clover waves me quiet with her hand. "Shush. This is getting interesting."

I crouch down beneath her and press my ear against the crack.

Mum is snorting with laughter. "Are you really accusing me of flirting with Dan?"

"What's wrong with Dan?" Prue asks, her voice sharp.

"He's just not my type, that's all. He's too clean-cut. I've never been into safe men in baggy cords and button-down shirts."

"What is your type? Grubby."

"*Grubby?* He's your brother, for God's sake," Mum says. "Have you no family loyalty?"

Prue harrumphs like a horse. "Family loyalty? Don't make me laugh. I've been keeping Dave afloat for years. Who do you think paid his way through medical school before he dropped out?"

"Medical school?" I whisper to Clover.

She shrugs. "News to me."

"That would have been me, Syl*vie*." Prue drawls out the end of Mum's name. "And I paid for the bloody wedding when he jilted poor Simone."

I look at Clover again; her eyes are the size of saucers.

"Dave Marcus, heartbreaker," she whispers. "Who'd have thought? I mean —"

"Shh," I hiss. "I'm trying to listen."

"That would be the poor Simone who married Dave's best friend, Paudie, six months later," I hear Mum say. "The poor Simone who had been seeing Paudie all along—behind Dave's back. That *poor* Simone."

"All speculation," Prue says tightly. "It was never proven. And regardless, it's another in a long line of Dave's failures. He keeps making a mess of his life, time after time. Just look at him now. Working all hours to pay half of someone else's mortgage. It's pathetic."

"One day we'll buy the other half of the house off Art," Mum retorts, and from the ice in her voice I can tell she's about to snap. "And our financial affairs are none of your concern, Prue, so why don't you just keep your nose out of our private family business and worry about your own family?"

"My family is perfectly fine, thank you very much."

"Really? You seem to have conveniently forgotten about Denis's comfort eating. He's going to be the size of an elephant soon, unless you do something about it."

"There's nothing wrong with Denis." Prue sounds

outraged. "Nothing. He's been to the very best dieticians and child psychologists. He does *not* comfort eat. How dare you!"

"I've found him in the kitchen almost every night, Prue. Wolfing down slices of bread or biscuits."

"Stop! I don't believe you. You're just saying that because your own life is such a mess. Your parenting skills are appalling and you have a boyfriend who can't commit. If Dave really loved you, he'd ask you to marry him. And as for having children with two different fathers, talk about irresponsible. If you ask me—"

"That's it," I hiss. I've been getting more and more angry, but this is the final straw.

Clover tries to grab my arm, but I'm too quick for her. I storm into the kitchen and go to stand beside Mum. "Mum's right," I tell Prue. "Denis is always eating. I've seen him too. Mum's not lying. And for your information, Dave is forever proposing to her. Mum's just not ready to get married again yet. She needs some time after Dad and everything. Isn't that right, Mum?" (The bit about Dave proposing isn't true, but everything else is.)

Mum just stares at me, her face twisted up. She looks angry and upset. Her hands are balled into fists, and I can tell she's trying not to cry.

"Mum," I say again, more gently, but she runs out of the room.

"Sylvie!" Prue shouts at her disappearing back. "I'm sorry. I was out of order."

Mum pounds up the stairs, and a few seconds later her bedroom door slams shut.

Prue starts to follow her, but I put a hand on her arm. "It's probably best to leave her alone."

Prue collapses onto a chair. She puts her head in her hands and starts sobbing. Oh, my God. They're both crazy.

"Prue?" Clover says gently.

She lifts her head. "I'm so sorry. I shouldn't have been so hard on Sylvie. She just winds me up so much sometimes." She hiccups through her tears. "She makes me feel so boring and pedestrian. Everything about her is more interesting — her job, her clothes, her friends. I wish my own life were a bit more exciting. I thought having a few drinks the other night might help, but I just felt really ill the next morning and ended up with a stain on one of my favorite tops." She sobs again.

"If it's any consolation, I think you wind Sylvie up too," Clover says. "Look, it's not easy sharing a house with another family — especially a family that's as crazy as ours. There are bound to be disagreements."

"Here." I hand Prue a paper towel. Luckily, she doesn't believe in wearing makeup; otherwise she'd have mascara running down her face, with all the waterworks.

"Thanks," she murmurs, flashing me a teary smile. "She's done such a good job with you, Amy. Even as a lone parent."

I don't really like the way she says *lone parent* — it makes Mum sound like a charity case — but I let it slide. I don't think she means it in a bad way.

"Being a parent is so hard," she says. "I love Denis, but I don't find him easy. Sometimes I'd just like to hand him back. Isn't that dreadful?"

"He's a good kid," Clover says kindly. "Smart too. He'll grow out of the weird behavior."

Prue smiles through her tears. "Thanks, Clover. I do hope you're right."

♥ Chapter 21

The following morning, I find Gramps sitting on a deck chair in the greenhouse reading the *Irish Independent*.

"So this is where you've been hiding," I say.

"It's like a zoo in there." He points at the house with the top of his newspaper.

"No kidding." I sit on the edge of a red-brick potting shelf.

There's a loud scraping noise outside, and we both look over. It's Kit. He's pulling a huge terra-cotta pot with a giant sunflower in it across the patio. The flower must be about four meters tall — its head is as big as a tire.

Gramps smiles. "Esther told me about Kit and his sunflowers. He feeds them seaweed."

"Have you been speaking to her again?" I ask, very surprised. "I thought you said she tried to kill you."

Gramps looks sheepish. "Ah, well, I may have exaggerated. She apologized for all that, anyway, said she got a bit carried away."

"But I don't understand. Did she explain why she did it?"

"No. She wants to come over. To talk. But I've asked her not to." He sighs. "There's no point. She made it perfectly clear how she feels about me the other night. And who knows what she might do to me this time!"

"Gramps, maybe you should see her. Clear the air. I'll come with you if you like, to keep you safe."

He smiles. "Thanks, Amy. But to be honest, she always was a tricky one. Full of life, but if you crossed her . . ." He draws a finger across his throat and whistles. "I'm sixty-five; I just want an easy life. She's a wonderful woman, but—" He shrugs. "You, on the other hand, have your whole life ahead of you, so go and talk to the young man with the sunflower; I know you're itching to."

I smile, my cheeks burning. "See you later, Gramps."

* * *

Kit has disappeared around the corner of the house, so I follow him. I gasp when I see what's there. A dozen towering sunflowers—some at least three meters tall—are standing along the side wall; their heads, supported by solid, slightly furry stalks, are tilted toward the gentle morning sun.

Some of the flower heads are turning to seed, and I run my fingers over the nubby roughness of the only one within reach. There's a bark to my right; it's coming from the maze. I've been itching to explore it since we got here, and now's my chance. And if that's Jack barking, then Kit's bound to be with him. My heart *thump-thump-thumps* just thinking about him.

I walk through the gate, feeling a little nervous at seeing him again, and come to a stop in front of the neatly pruned gap in the hedge—the entrance to the maze.

Jack barks once more, as though drawing me on.

But how do I navigate the maze? Then I remember what Mrs. Sketchberry told us in classics, about the labyrinth of Crete and the Minotaur. Apparently, in most mazes the walls are connected, so if you put one of your hands on the wall and keep it in place—never lifting it—you'll eventually find the exit.

I really hope it's as easy as that.

I start to walk, trailing my right hand along the scratchy hedge. It's giving off a bitter, tangy smell that catches at the back of my throat.

Jack barks again. I walk on more quickly, taking a few more turns. The walls seem to be getting taller with each step and the path narrower. The hedge presses in on either side, catching my shoulders.

It's completely airless in here, and the smell is becoming overpowering. I must be nearing the center by now, surely — but maybe Mrs. Sketchberry was wrong. Maybe I'm completely off track. Lost. I should have never stepped inside.

Then I hear Jack to my right. He seems to be luring me farther in.

Speeding up, I follow the noise. But what if Kit's on his way out of the maze? I don't want to get stuck in here by myself — trapped and alone until I die from heat exposure and dehydration. I pat my pocket: nothing. My mobile must be in my room, and in here no one will hear my screams. The hedge might grow up and over my head, sealing me beneath its boughs, like something out of Harry Potter. The way it's towering over me, it really feels as if it could.

OK, now my imagination is running away with itself. There's no such thing as an enchanted hedge.

Crunch! Hang on, what's that? I hear it again, louder this time. It sounds like a twig breaking. Maybe it's a mouse — or even worse, a rat. My mind goes into overdrive. There's something in here with me, following me. What if all that Minotaur stuff is true? Maybe a bull-headed maze monster really is after me!

I begin to run, dashing around the corners completely randomly, not caring whether I turn left or right, just wanting to get away from whoever or whatever is chasing me. And then suddenly I stop dead.

Miraculously, I've found the center of the maze. I bend at the waist, panting; my hands rest on the tops of my thighs as I gasp for air. When I look up, I see a green metal bench and an old stone pond, its curved sides covered in moss.

"Amy, are you all right? Why were you running away from me?"

Kit runs out from the maze behind me. He stops to catch his breath, his chest thrust out, hands on hips, and a T-shirt dripping with fresh sweat. Jack is right behind him, his pink tongue hanging out.

I stagger over to the bench and flop down. Yikes, what can I tell him? I can hardly say, "I thought I was being chased by a Greek monster," can I? "I'm claustrophobic," I say, improvising. "I get panic attacks in lifts or . . . um . . . mazes, apparently, as I've just found out."

He nods silently, seeming (to my delight) to accept my lame explanation.

A drop of sweat trickles down my back, making me wiggle. I gaze longingly at the pond. The water looks cool and inviting.

"Water's clean," Kit says, reading my mind. "Stick yer feet in if you like."

I stare down at my hot, dusty feet, kick off my flip-flops, and dip a toe in the water. It's heavenly. I sit on the edge of the pool, then take a step in.

Whoosh! My feet go from under me and I end up on my bum, water up to my stomach. I scream, putting my hands down to steady myself. The granite feels weedy and slimy under my fingers. No wonder I slipped. I feel so stupid.

A grin splits Kit's face and he starts to chuckle. He's even cuter when he's laughing; I want to reach up and touch the little crinkles at the sides of his eyes.

"What?" I demand, mortified. "It could happen to anyone." I splash some water at him. "Besides, it's lovely. You should try it."

"When it's hot, sometimes I have a soak to cool off."

I picture Kit splashing around in this very pond,

starkers. I blush, and then to distract his attention from my tomato face, I say, "Prove it."

Kit sits down on the edge of the pool, slides his feet out of his flip-flops, pulls off his grubby T-shirt, and steps carefully into the pool, leaving his shorts on. The water only reaches his mid-calves.

He sits down beside me, soaking his shorts, leans back against the pool's edge, and shuts his eyes. "Satisfied?" he asks.

I check him out. He's broad and solid, more heavily built than Seth, and he's so close I can smell his fresh sweat. "Oh, yes," I murmur.

He opens his eyes and catches me staring at him.

I whisk my eyes away. "Water's lovely, isn't it?" I start to feel embarrassed. "But I'd better get back."

I try to stand up but lurch forward, falling on top of Kit. I give his nose quite a whack with the palm of my hand. "Sorry." I try to scramble away from him, but I slip again and end up sitting on his lap instead. *Morto!*

He puts his hands around my waist. "Easy, tiger."

His face is inches from mine; his strong hands are still holding my waist, and I can almost feel the texture of his skin through my T-shirt. My heart starts to pound, and I suddenly have this overwhelming urge to kiss him.

"You OK?" he asks, taking his hands away.

"Yes," I say, and then start to gabble with nerves. "Quite fine. A bit wet, of course, but otherwise unharmed." I stand up, holding on to the side of the pond this time to steady myself, and then sit down carefully on the ledge.

Kit says nothing, his eyes fixed on mine. The silence begins to feel uncomfortable.

"Better head back." I look away to break the gaze.

"Aye." He steps out and holds his hand out to me.

As soon as our skin connects—*zing!* It's like an electric current running up my arm, and I almost gasp. His palm feels rough and hard, and his hand is much bigger than mine; his fingers reach the top of my wrist.

When I'm out of the pool and standing beside him, he drops my hand. "Best follow me," he says. "Don't want you getting lost."

The path is too narrow for us to walk side by side, so I follow behind him, Jack trotting along behind us. We both drip onto the dusty path.

At the entrance I say, "Sorry for getting you so wet."

" 'S OK." He gazes at me with those intense eyes. "What were you looking for, anyway?"

"Sorry?"

"In the maze. Were you looking for me?" From the smile on his lips, I can tell he's pleased at the thought.

I swallow and look away, hoping I don't look too guilty. "No! I just wanted to test out the wall-following rule. You know, the one about keeping one hand on the wall. Our classics teacher told us about it."

He winks at me. "Just as well you found me, then. The walls of this maze aren't connected. You'd have gotten lost, and the Lough Ine Minotaur would have eaten you." He grins.

"You know the story?"

"Aye."

"Amy!" Clover is shouting from the French doors at the back of the house. "Lover boy's on the phone from Italy. Quick!" She's waving the house phone in the air.

I turn to say good-bye to Kit, but he's already disappeared.

Taking the phone from Clover, who's making kissing noises at me, I walk inside. I don't want anyone to hear my conversation, so I lock myself in the downstairs loo and sit on the closed toilet seat. "Seth? Are you still there?"

"Hi, Amy. What took you so long?"

"I was checking out the maze." I'm about to tell him about Kit, but I stop, aware that my feelings for Kit might not be strictly platonic. "What's the weather like over there?" I ask instead.

"Sweltering. We've given up on sightseeing; it's too hot."

"I'm sure that will suit Jin just fine. She can show off her tan in her dental-floss bikini."

Seth says nothing.

I give a snide laugh, then plow on. "Not that you'd be interested, of course — in her big jelly puppies, flopping around in her tiny bikini tops." *Amy, just stop talking*, I tell myself. "Seth. Seth? Are you still there? I didn't mean it. About the puppies. Ignore me."

"Amy, what were you just saying? I couldn't make it out. Something about puppies. Sorry, this line is terrible."

Thank you, god of teenage motormouths. He didn't even hear my green-eyed delirium.

"Nothing important," I trill. "Just talking about Dad's new dog. Dad's arriving on Tuesday. With

Shelly. Mum's going to go even more mental once they get here. Anyway, thanks for ringing. I miss you."

"I miss you too. And Amy?"

·"Yes?"

The phone goes dead. Typical. And then suddenly I remember — it's July 12, Seth's birthday. I meant to sing *"Tanti Auguri,"* the Italian version of "Happy Birthday," to him. I found it on YouTube last night and learned the words specially. But I got a bit distracted by Kit and the maze and everything. I'd like to ring Seth back, but I don't have the number. *"Siúcra!"* I mutter.

I'm damp and uncomfortable, so I stamp upstairs to change. I struggle grumpily out of my sodden jeans and knickers, kicking them into the corner of the room, and put on dry ones. Seth doesn't deserve such a useless girlfriend.

♥ Chapter 22

Clover lies back and hits her head on a rock. "What is it with this beach?" She rubs the back of her skull. "A beach isn't a beach without sand. We should have stayed at the other one."

We're sitting on a stony beach on the far side of the island, away from the noisy babies who invaded the sandy beach with their buckets and spades.

"We shouldn't be relaxing on a beach, anyway," I remind her. "We're supposed to be working. The new agony aunt pages won't wait, you know."

Clover laughs. "You sound just like Saffy. Scary biscuits. Why does everyone keep going on about work? Work, smirk. Gramps is just as bad."

"Why?"

"He keeps going on at me about college. It's *très* boring."

"What *are* you up to in September? Are you going to take another year off?"

Clover's really clever — she never did a tap of work at school but still managed to get accepted to study English and history of art at Trinity College, which is pretty good going.

"I haven't decided. I might see if I can defer another year. The magazine's keen to keep me on. As long as Saskia doesn't nab my job, that is." She bites her lip.

"Can't you do both? It's only English and art history."

She throws a pebble at my feet. "Less of that, Beanie. English and history of art are both hard, I'll have you know. What are you going to do, then? Rocket science?"

"Maybe. I *am* good at math."

Clover puts on a smug voice. "Hello, I'm Amy Sylvie Mabel Green. I'm an absolute genius at math; I know pi to ten places after the decimal point, and I'm not afraid to use it."

I laugh nervously. The thing is, I do know pi to ten decimal places. (It's 3.1415926535.) I also know it in binary numbers. Well, a bit of it — 11.0010 — and I know it's 3.24 in hexadecimals. (Don't ask!) I have a bit of a thing about pi. It's just so interesting and really important too. Loads of math and science formulas depend on it.

"But seriously," I say, "what are you going to do about college?"

"We'll see," she says noncommittally. "But speaking of the magazine, how's Mills getting on with her American boy?"

"OK. She's doing her best to attract his attention, and at least he talks to her now, but nothing's really happened yet." I read Mills's latest e-mail last night. She sounds a bit fed up. "And Marlon and Betty are driving her crazy."

Clover snorts. "I'm not surprised. With any luck they'll be gobbled up by Miami gators. That's what the Miami Mafia does with all the murdered bodies." She pulls her laptop out of her bag and opens it up. "I suppose we'd better get cracking."

Just then a stone lands inches away from Clover's head.

"Hey!" She swings around.

Denis is staring down at us.

"Denis, you little —" Clover stops herself. "Denis, that wasn't very nice. Get down here."

To my surprise, he actually does what she says, standing in front of her, a scowl on his face.

"What do you say?" she asks.

"Sorry I missed," he says.

Clover shakes her head. "You're not making things easy for yourself, Denis. I don't know why we bother even talking to you."

He wanders off toward the water, picks up a huge stone, and chucks it in. The splash soaks our legs.

"Denis!" I yell.

"Get over here!" Clover shouts in a steely voice even I wouldn't mess with.

Denis lumbers over, his feet dragging through the stones. "What?"

"Why are you being so horrible? And stop scowling at me. You'd be very handsome if you'd only stop with the faces."

Denis looks surprised.

"Now, apologize properly," Clover says firmly.

"Sorry, Clover," he murmurs.

And you know something? I think he means it.

At ten o'clock that evening, I finally get around to ringing Seth back. He rang Haven House when Clover and I were at the beach and left the number. I hope Esther won't be too cross about one emergency phone call to Italy.

A female voice answers. *"Pronto."*

"Hello, I'm looking for Seth Stone."

"Oh, hi!" says a perky English voice. "This is Jin. You must be Amy. Seth's told me so much about you; I feel like we're best friends. He's been expecting you. Hang on a mo'."

The line goes quiet, and in the background I hear her shout, "Seth!"

So that's Jin. I instantly feel all prickly. Best friends? When she's clearly after Seth? How dare she? I shouldn't have bothered ringing at all.

"Hi, Amy." Seth sounds very chirpy. He's probably just stolen a passing kiss from Jin. I bet she's in the room now, laughing at me. *Stupid Amy, doesn't she know she's no match for my Jin jelly puppies?* "You got the message, then."

"Yes," I say tightly. "But I'm sorry to interrupt you."

"Interrupt me? Are you OK? You sound a bit funny. And you didn't call me back earlier."

"I was busy — and besides, I didn't have the number then, remember?"

"You could have sent an e-mail — or are you too busy to e-mail your sad and lonely boyfriend on his birthday?"

I snort. "Get a grip, Seth. You're hardly sad and lonely, are you?"

"Sorry?"

"I think you know exactly what I mean. Jin."

"Jin?" He laughs. "We're just friends."

"Don't give me that. She's a boyfriend predator. She's been moving in on you from day one, admit it. And stop talking to her about me. It's creepy."

Seth laughs again. "Amy, you're being paranoid. There's nothing going on between me and Jin. In fact, she's got—" He breaks off. "What? Oh, right. Amy, I'm really sorry, Jin's mum wants to use the phone. I have to go. But I'll ring you back in half an hour. OK?"

"Don't bother. Actually, don't bother contacting me ever again. From now on, we are officially over, Seth—understand? You hop along. Go and play with Jin."

"Amy, you're overreacting. I can't talk about this right now, but—"

"Why? Is Jin's mum cute too?"

"Amy! Yuck, what a thought. She's ancient. No way, José. I'm not interested in anyone else, I swear. Look, can we talk about this later?"

"No. I'm sorry, Seth, but now *I* have to get off the phone. Please don't ring me again—I mean it." I click off the phone.

Tears start to stream down my face, and I have a lump the size of a field-hockey ball in my throat.

What have I just done?

♥ Chapter 23

"No!" I scream at Mum. "I won't be bloody reasonable. Why can't I go to Cork with Clover? It's so unfair. Dad won't be here for hours."

"I'm sorry, Amy, but you just can't, and that's final. Deal with it. And if you don't stop swearing at me, you're going straight to your room."

"I'm thirteen; you can't send me to my room."

"Yes, I can. You may be thirteen, young lady, but I'm still your mother."

"Fine, then. I'll go to my bloody room. Happily. Anything to get away from you. I HATE YOU!" I storm out of the kitchen, stomp up the stairs and into my room, slamming the door behind me, and flop down on the bed.

Clover stares at me, the lip gloss in her hand frozen in midair. "Ah, Mama say no," she says.

I fold my arms tightly across my chest. "Mum's being a complete cow, and I don't want to talk about it."

"She does have a point. Your dad and Shelly might be a bit miffed if you're in Cork on the first night of their hols. They're only here for a few days."

I glare up at her. "Not you as well. I thought you'd be on my side."

"I *am* on your side, Beanie." Clover sits down on the edge of the bed and tries to give me a hug, but I shrug her arms away. She gets up and swings her overnight bag onto her shoulder. "I guess I'll see you tomorrow evening. Look, I'm sorry about all this—"

"No, you're not! You're delighted. You can't wait to get away from me. Oh, you're nice enough when you need me, aren't you, Clover? When there's a *Goss* letter that needs answering or an article you need help with. I'm *always* helping people, you and Mum and Dave—but what about *me*?" I point at my chest. "What about *my* needs?"

The edges of Clover's mouth twitch—she'd better not be laughing at me. But she just sighs. "Beanie, you're not making much sense. It's not my fault you can't come to Cork with me."

"You could have reasoned with Mum — said you couldn't talk to Efa Valentine without me. I helped you prepare the questions, Clover, remember?"

"I know you did, and I tried to talk to her, believe me. Sylvie can be very stubborn when she wants to be. It runs in the family." She looks at me pointedly, but I ignore her. "Anyway, she's made up her mind on this one. I really am sorry."

"No, you're not. You're dying to meet Efa and ask her all my questions." I grab at her bag. "Give them to me."

"What?" She presses the bag against her side with her elbow.

"Go on, give me the questions. They're mine."

"Don't be so unreasonable. I wrote them too."

"Liar!" I snatch at her bag again.

"Stop it! What's gotten into you?" She pushes me away.

I gasp. Now she's done it. "You just hit me," I say.

"I did not."

"Yes, you did. Just like this." I push her back, hard. She stumbles toward the door and whacks her arm against the door handle.

"What the hell's wrong with you?" She rubs the reddened flesh above her elbow. "That hurt." She pulls open the door. "I'm going now — I hope you'll be in a better mood when I get back."

"Don't bother coming back!" I yell. "No one will miss you."

She leaves in silence, without turning around.

I collapse on the bed, utterly miserable. What is wrong with me? Why was I so mean to Clover? I start to cry; big salty tears run down my cheeks. I have this huge ball of tension swirling inside me, like a black hole gobbling up everything in its path, and I just spat a whole fur ball of it at Clover.

I have to catch her before she leaves; tell her I'm sorry. Sitting up, I wipe away the tears with my sleeve. I run downstairs and into the kitchen, shouting, "Clover. Clover!"

Mum's on her mobile. "Yes, of course," she's saying. "I understand." She puts up a finger, as if to say, *Wait there a second.* I ignore her and sprint outside.

An engine is starting up, and I dash down to the beach in time to see Dave and Clover in one of the boats, speeding toward the harbor. They chug happily through the sloppy little waves, oblivious to my shouts and waves.

Shoulders dropped practically to my feet, I slope back to the house to get my mobile and try calling Clover. Nothing's going right today.

Mum's still standing in the kitchen, waiting for me, Evie jiggling on her hip. Mum's sunglasses are resting on top of her newly sun-bleached hair. She's wearing a red top, white jeans, and flip-flops. She actually looks quite nice. Pity she's such a witch.

"I was just talking to your dad," she says. "And if you hadn't flounced off like that, you could have spoken to him in person. Shelly's not great. Apparently, she had a bit of a scare last night. A bleed. Your dad says it's probably nothing, but they don't want to be too far from the maternity hospital, just in case, so they're going to stay in Dublin."

"Are they coming down tomorrow?"

"No, they're not coming down at all."

I perk up. "Does that mean I can go to Cork with Clover?"

Mum looks at me in surprise. "I've already said no, Amy. No means no. It's too late now. And, frankly, you've been so rude to me all morning, I think it's best if you stay here and think about your behavior. You can help me with the babies."

The black hole starts churning again, faster and faster. This is so unjust. "In your dreams," I say. "Find another slave. I'm going out." I storm out of the door.

She follows me. "Amy Green, if you leave this island, you're in big trouble."

I spin around on my heels. "The boats are both being used, so how am I going to do that? Swim? We're on Alcatraz, didn't you know? But at least in San Francisco the water might be warmer, so there'd be some hope of escape without contracting hypothermia."

"If you didn't get eaten by the crocodiles and sharks first," Mum calls after me. "Oh, for God's sake, Amy — come back inside."

I march down the garden and take a sharp right, out of her sight. Then I notice the old stone boathouse. Kit. At least *he*'ll be pleased to see me. I hope.

Seth's face floats in front of my eyes. I blink it away and try not to think about last night's phone call. Why is everything such a mess?

♥ Chapter 24

I knock on the bottle-green door of the boathouse.
Nothing. White canvas blinds have been pulled
down in the windows, so I walk toward the far end
of the building. A crumbling stone ramp runs down
toward the sea, and at the top of it, instead of doors,
there's a huge sheet-glass window.

It takes a few moments for my eyes to adjust to
the light, but when they do, I almost fall over in
surprise. Hundreds of shards of colored glass have
been suspended from the ceiling of the boathouse.
Pressed up against the window, they seem to be floating in the air.

I gaze at the rainbow of color. The sun peeps out
from behind the clouds, and immediately the whole

window is lit up by a spectacular wall of dancing light, like a giant kaleidoscope.

Some of the pieces start to spin, and Kit appears at the window, making me jump. Spotting me, he waves down and mouths, "Other door."

When I get back around to the green door, it's already open.

"That you knocking?" he asks when I go in. "Thought I heard something, but I was listening to my iPod. Coming in?"

I nod eagerly and step into the open-plan room. "That glass is amazing," I say. "What is it?"

"Mam's mobile."

"Was she an artist?"

"Nah. She just liked glass."

He leads me past a beaten-up leather armchair, with an old brass telescope standing beside it and a small kitchenette just beyond. Hundreds of books are stacked in towering piles against the walls. There's a double bed to our left. It isn't made: the white duvet is bunched at the bottom and a book lies open on the sheet. On the cover is a photo of a guy sitting on an old-fashioned minibus.

I read the title: *Into the Wild*.

"You like reading?" I ask.

"Sure."

"What kind of books?"

"Adventures, survival books, anything about the wilderness." He nods at the book on the bed. "That one's about a guy who runs away and camps out in this minibus in Alaska. Manages to live by eating plants and stuff. It's good. He dies at the end, though."

"Thanks for telling me."

He shrugs. "Says so on the first page. It's a true story."

"Oh." Then, not knowing what to say next, I study the glass mobile. "Can I touch it?"

"OK. But watch your fingers. The glass is sharp."

Now that I am closer to it, I can see that as well as the sharp slivers of glass, there are other shiny things: shards of mirror, a small hole bored in the top to secure them, and even a baby-size silver fork, polished until it gleams. And smooth, gentle curves of sea glass.

I touch a piece of blue glass. "This piece is so beautiful," I say, dazzled by the moody midnight color.

"Aye, it were Mam's favorite too. Murano glass from Venice. Like this." He passes me what looks like a crystal ball.

"What is it?" I ask, peering at the tiny woman trapped inside. She's sitting on a rock, her hair streaming out behind her, like a sheet of silk, and although she's no bigger than my thumb, her eyes look dark and hypnotic.

"Paperweight. Mam collected them. That one's of a selkie. Half woman, half seal. It's an old Celtic legend. Mam was into that kind of thing — said she could hear the voices of the O'Driscolls, who used to live on this island, when she dug the earth. Believed in fairies too."

"Fairies? Really?"

"Aye. Used to put a saucer of milk on all the windowsills at night to stop bad things happening to us. Said our house was on a fairy line."

"What did your dad think?"

He shrugs. "I don't think Da had time to be worrying about it. He spent most of his time trying to stop her hurting herself."

I stare at him. "What do you mean?"

"Nothing," he murmurs. "I shouldn't have said that. Stupid." He glances at his wristwatch. "Sorry, I have to get back to work. I'll see you around." And then he stands by the door, holding it open.

I feel awkward, embarrassed. I want to say something, to ask him more about his mum, but I can tell the subject is closed and that now he's trying to get rid of me. Our eyes connect. There's a sadness behind his gaze. I want to reach out and touch him, hold him, but instead I drag my eyes away. "Thanks for showing me the glass mobile," I say softly.

"No bother. See ya, Amy."

I walk out of the door and he closes it firmly behind me.

That evening I open my e-mail account and scan the in-box. There's nothing from Seth. I wasn't really expecting anything, not after our phone call, and I know it's not rational, but still I'm disappointed.

However, there is an e-mail from Mills:

Hi, Amy,

How's it going? Hope you're not missing Seth too much. Things over here are heating up, and I don't mean the weather!

Matt, the boy I was telling you about, has finally started to talk to me — properly — and he's so sweet and funny. He's really into Ireland and wants to hear all about living in Dublin and school and everything.

But stop the lights . . . I'm starting to like his best friend, Ed, more and more. He's cute and funny and a bit goofy, but in a nice way.

Now what do I do? Yikes!

No other news, really. The Costigans are out most evenings, so I've been hanging out with Marlon and Betty. Thrills and spills — not! Luckily, they are ridiculously easy to bribe (thank Clover for the tip!). But I'm not going to come home with much money at this rate, what with buying sweets for them and spending all my moolah at American Apparel.

Yowsers, Amy — clothes are way cheap over here, and it's so much fun rooting around in the bargain bins. Wish you were here to share my U.S. shopping experiences!

Miss you so much. Sob, sob. If it weren't for Matt and Ed, I'd be going loop da loop.

E-mail me immediately and tell me all the goss — has Seth written you any more super-swoony poems? Spill all.

Your bestest amiga,
Mills XXXXXXXXXXX

I sit back in my seat and think. What am I going to say? I've broken up with Seth, I've had a huge fight with Clover and Mum, and now even Kit doesn't want to talk to me. I'm basically a loser with no life. Tears spring into my eyes. Oh, no, there've been enough weeping willows around this place with Mum and Prue. This house must be cursed. I switch off the computer and stare into space for a few minutes, blinking back the tears.

"Amy?" Mum walks into the room.

"Don't worry — I'm going to bed." I run past her.

"Sleep well, Amy," she says to my back.

As if.

♥ Chapter 25

I sleep badly, tossing and turning all night. When I wake up, my face feels clammy and my hair's stuck to my forehead, as though I've been sweating. I brush it back with my hand and rub the sleep stickiness from the edges of my mouth.

And then I notice my knickers are damp. Last night I was too tired and irritable to change into my pajamas, so I climbed into bed in my T-shirt and underwear. I lie there in horror. No! I couldn't have wet myself during the night. I did that a couple of times when I was little. The last time was just after Dad moved out, when I was nine. But I'm thirteen now.

I roll over and pull back my duvet and stare at the bottom sheet. Nothing. Then I sit on the edge of my bed and pull down my knickers. There are spots of dark-red blood on the cotton. I start to freak out. What if I'm ill? Then it dawns on me. My period.

Finally!

I start to feel all wobbly. What do I do now? I don't have anything with me — I wasn't expecting this to happen on holiday — and I refuse to speak to Mum. Clover would know what to do, but she's in a hotel somewhere in Cork city.

I look at my watch. Five past seven. Clover will kill me for waking her up (she likes her sleep), but it's an emergency.

"Yello? This had better be important," Clover says groggily.

"Clover, it's me. Sorry for ringing so early."

"What's wrong, Beanie? Have you got a cold? You sound like Mr. Snuffleupagus."

"Mr. who?"

"The elephant from *Sesame Street*. Never mind that — what's up, jelly tot?"

It's such a relief to find that Clover is actually speaking to me after the way I treated her yesterday, I start to cry.

"Beanie? Are you OK? Say something. What's happened? You're seriously freaking me out here."

"I got my period!" I wail. "And I don't know what to do."

"Congrats — that's cool, babes. Told you it wouldn't be long. Don't be upset, it's all easy peasy. But where's Sylvie? Isn't she there?"

"I shouted at her last night and now she hates me."

"She doesn't hate you. Don't be such a moo. Anyway, it wasn't your fault. You were clearly riddled with PMS."

"PMS?"

"Premenstrual syndrome. In fact, I should have spotted it. *That's* why you've been in such a bad mood for the last few days. It's your hormones. They've been hopping around like jumping beans. Right, as soon as I've got this Efa interview in the bag, I'm going to hop in the car and get down to you lickety-split. I'm taking you shopping in Skibbereen to celebrate."

"To buy what, exactly?" I ask wryly. "A saucepan? Or a pair of green farmer's wellies?" (The town isn't exactly inundated with cool shops.)

She laughs. "I see your point. Not exactly New York, is it? Don't worry, we'll find something. And we can stock up on sani stuff at the drugstore too."

"But what will I do till then?"

"Darn, my stuff's all in my makeup bag here. Maybe Sylvie has something. Or you could use loo paper. Layer it into a pad. I'll be as quick as I can, promise."

After saying good-bye to Clover, I stick my head around the door. All clear. Clutching a clean pair of knickers and my black jeans to my stomach, I run to the bathroom and lock the door behind me. I sit on the toilet and take off my soiled pants.

Then I layer toilet paper in my hand, weaving it backward and forward into a pad, the way Clover suggested, before popping the wad into my fresh knickers, pulling them up, and stepping into my black jeans. At least if I do leak, no one will see.

I ball up the old knickers, wrap them in toilet paper, and put them in the bin. Finally, I wash my hands and walk back to my bedroom, trying not to waddle like a penguin.

Mum comes into my room an hour later. "Are you coming down for breakfast, Amy?"

Keeping my eyes firmly fixed on my book, I shake my head.

"OK, then," she says gently. "I'll bring something up. You probably feel like resting. It's a big day for you."

I look up. "What do you mean?"

"I found your knickers when I was putting Evie's nappy in the bin."

"Oh." How humiliating.

"You don't need to throw them out. A bit of Shout will deal with it." She sits down on the bed. "Look, let's just forget about yesterday, OK? It was probably just a touch of PMS. I get it too."

I roll my eyes. "I've noticed." Sometimes Mum sits and cries at the kitchen table for no reason. Other times she puts Evie's Onesies in my chest of drawers. Am I going to turn into a basket case every single month, like Mum, now? I hope not!

She laughs. "Are you all right? Do you need some pads? I have some Always in my bag. Or do you want to try tampons?"

I gulp. This is all so cringe-inducing. "The Always will be fine. Thanks. I'm going to Skibbereen with Clover later; I can go to a drugstore then."

"OK. Remind me to give you some money." She gives me a hug and kisses the top of my head. "Oh, Amy," she says into my hair.

"Mum!"

"Sorry, sorry. It's just . . ." She tails off, her eyes moist. "You're growing up so quickly. I still remember the day you were born. All that hair — like a little brown mop stuck to your head." She shakes her head and sighs.

"Sylvie!" Dave yells up the stairs. "Have you seen the baby wipes?"

She stands up. "Duty calls. I'll be up with toast in a few minutes. Jam?"

I nod.

She lingers at the door for a second, staring at me. She opens her mouth to say something, then closes it again.

"Sylvie!" Dave hollers again. "The poo's going everywhere."

"I'll be right there!" she shouts back. She smiles at me. "I love you so much, Amy. You're my special firstborn, and now you're a woman."

I nod, willing her to go away. She's so embarrassing.

"Sylvie! Evie just put her hand in it. Help!"

Mum winces. "Better run."

♥ Chapter 26

I'm walking into the Church Café in Skibbereen with Clover for lunch, all ready to get the lowdown on the Efa interview, when I spot a familiar face sitting at a nearby table. "Gramps! What are you doing here?"

The top of his bald head goes scarlet. "Hello, Amy. Clover. I'm just . . . well, I'm just . . .." he falters.

Then I see Esther. She's sitting opposite him, smiling at us. "Hi, girls," she says.

She looks really nice. Her long white hair is hanging in a thick braid down her back, the end decorated with a silk sunflower, and she's wearing a white linen shirt with a wide leather belt and a swishy brown suede skirt.

"Love the belt," Clover says, glaring at her. "But isn't it a bit young for you?"

Clover is very protective of Gramps, and she clearly hasn't forgiven Esther for trying to kill him.

Esther laughs easily. "I'm glad you like it; I got it in Milan. Would you like to join us?" She gestures at the table. It looks a bit on the small side for four.

I glance at Gramps. He's frowning.

"Love to," Clover says, undaunted. She pulls a chair over and squashes in beside Esther, pushing Esther's chair out of the way rather rudely and elbowing her in the side.

I mouth, "Sorry," at Gramps and sit down beside him.

"So," Clover says to Esther while giving her a sickly sweet smile, "you've decided murder isn't the answer, then."

"Clover!" Gramps says.

Esther throws her head back and gives a belly laugh. "I suppose I have. Death is horribly overrated." She turns to Gramps. "Like I said, I'm so sorry, Len. And I must say, it's very brave of you to agree to meet me for lunch. After the rats and everything."

"I was curious," Gramps says with a shrug. "And I reckoned I'd be fairly safe somewhere called the *Church* Café."

Esther smiles. "You'd be surprised. I know the owners very well. I'm sure I could persuade them to slip something in your sandwich." She gives Gramps a wink. "One of them is Kit Harper's aunt, in fact."

"Kit from Haven House?" I ask quickly.

"You've met him?" she says.

I nod. "I've talked to him as well. He seems nice."

She seems taken aback. "Really? He usually doesn't say much. He can be a bit . . . how can I put this? Abrupt. He hasn't been the same since his mum—" She breaks off. "Well, since she died. May was the gardener at Haven House before Kit; he's inherited her green thumb. They were very close, Kit and May; used to do everything together. More like best friends than mother and son. Her death was a real tragedy. Nearly wiped the poor lad out. He's a bit of a loner now. His dad's worried about him—but what can you do? There'll always be a job for him at Haven, although he could do so much more with his life." She sighs. "Maybe I shouldn't have interfered, but it seemed like the right thing to do, and I'm a woman of impulse."

"That you are," Gramps agrees with a grin. "You always were kindhearted, Esther. And a good little dancer too, if I recall."

"You were no slouch yourself, Len." She beams at him, then turns to us. "Len and I go back a long way, girls. To cut a long story short, he broke my heart. Stood me up and then disappeared for a week without a word. I was distraught." She breaks off and stares down at her hands, then looks up again. "So I decided to get revenge. I thought it would help — but I felt worse afterward, not better. So I'm here today to apologize. I feel a little foolish, to be frank."

Gramps is staring at her, his mouth open. "But, Esther, I left a message. With one of your friends at the nurses' home. Rosalind, I think her name was. I made her swear she'd give it to you."

Esther snorts. "Rosaleen, you mean? She was hardly a friend. She had a thing for you, Len — didn't you know?"

He shakes his head. "So you never got my message?"

"No. I thought you'd just stood me up."

"I'm so sorry." He reaches out and takes her hand in his. "I've never forgotten you, Esther." He gazes at her, his blue eyes sparkling with warmth. "Never."

I jump to my feet. "Clover, I just remembered: Mum wants us back for lunch."

Clover looks at me, her nose wrinkling. "She does?"

"Yes!" I pull her up by the arm. "Nice to meet you again, Esther. Enjoy your lunch."

"What was that all about?" Clover asks outside, rubbing her arm.

"Everyone deserves a second chance," I say. "Even Esther. And did you see the way Gramps was looking at her? Methinks we were getting in the way."

We have lunch at Field's Café instead. As we're walking back toward the car, Clover's mobile rings.

She answers it. "Yello? Oh, hi, Saffy. . . . Really? That's great to hear. . . . Efa was lovely; I'll write it up later and file it this evening. . . . What? . . . Poor Saskia. . . . Yes, I always travel with my passport, just in case. You taught me that. . . . No! Are you serious? . . . Sounds great. . . . Actually, I know Ria. Yes . . ." She grins from ear to ear. "Miami? First class? Absa-doodle-oodle! I'll get back to you within the hour, I promise."

Clover throws her mobile into her bag and does a little dance on the pavement in the car park. "Mi-a-mi," she sings, rotating her fists in front of her and wiggling her bum. "Mi-a-mi. I'm going to Mi-a-mi."

I look at her expectantly. "What's happened?"

"Efa's people were very impressed with me. Said I handled the interview very professionally and had obviously done my research." Clover blows on her fingers and rubs them on her shoulder. "Remember the girl I was telling you about, Saskia Davenport?"

"The journo-vamp who's after your job?"

"The very one. Well, she fell up some steps at a book launch last night. Broke two fingers and sprained her ankle. I have no idea how you fall *up* steps, but Saffy said champagne and high heels were involved. She said Saskia's hopping mad about missing the interview. Ha!"

"When are you going?"

"Tomorrow." She squeals and flaps her hands — but then her face drops. "Oh, *póg*! What on earth am I going to pack? I need to dress to impress. Matt Munroe. Imagine it, Beanie!" She sighs happily. "I can die a happy woman. Oh, and with Ria Costigan involved in the PR and everything, I might even get to see Mills. Fun!"

It's a brilliant opportunity for Clover, but I'm starting to feel pretty low. "Tomorrow? For how long?"

"Barely three days. A lot of palaver for one interview, but that's showbiz. Ah, Beans, why the long face?"

I shrug. "Tomorrow's Thursday, so you won't be back till Sunday. That's three whole days on my ownio. Plus you'll get to see Mills. How unfair is that?"

"I really am sorry. But we're not leaving here until

Monday. At least we'll have one more day together."
Then her face lights up. "Hang on, I have an idea.
Does Sylvie still bring all the passports and birth cer-
tificates with her on holidays in case the house burns
down?"

"Yes." Suddenly it dawns on me. "You're going
to bring me too! Oh, Clover, please, please, please,
please!" I say, jumping up and down in excitement.

She gives me a little smile. "I'm not saying a thing
till I've conversed with the olds."

"Clover!" I thump her arm. "You're impossible."

"Jeepers, are you determined to scar me for life?
Quit attacking me, Beanie — or you're off the *Goss* for
good. Speaking of which, I have an easy peasy *Goss*
letter for you to help me with when we get home. I
need to file it before tomorrow. You in?"

"Yes — as long as you let me come to Miami."

"That's blackmail."

I smile. "You've taught me everything I know."

♥ Chapter 27

That evening Clover and I finally get to work on the agony-aunt letter. We do some research on the Internet, and then Clover dictates a response while I type it up and add my own bits to the text. As the e-mail's a few weeks old, I get the feeling that Clover has been holding on to this one especially.

> Dear Clover,
>   I think I'm going mad. I recently started getting my period, and I feel so grumpy and exhausted just before and during, like I'm getting the flu or something.

I keep snapping at my little sister (she's five) for no reason, and today I threw a Barbie horse at her 'cause she was annoying me so much. It hit her on the cheek and left a red mark. Mum sent me to my room. My sis has a bruise now, and I feel really bad.

Is it normal to feel like this? Do other girls go crazy during their time of the month? Do you have any advice?

Please help!

Becs, 14, Sligo

Dear Becs,

First of all, please don't worry; you're not going mad! It's quite normal to get tired and feel awful before your period. Some girls get zits; others feel heavy and bloated. You are not alone — a lot of girls (myself included!) get very grumpy and irritable before and during their period; this is called PMS or PMT — premenstrual syndrome or premenstrual tension.

It's linked to low hormone levels, although there hasn't been all that much research done on it. Personally, I think we need far more female

scientists to straighten out the male boffins and *That's my bit!*
do research on things that really matter, like PMS!

I find two things help: eat small snacks at short intervals during the day, including nips of chocolate (any excuse!), to keep your blood sugar up and give you energy; and exercise. Yes, shopping with the girls does count!

Try to rest if you're feeling tired and grotty — I find curling up in bed with a good book can make me feel better. Maybe you could listen to your favorite music or take a bubble bath with your fave mag (the *Goss*, of course!). Or ring a good friend and have a bit of a chat — anything that helps take your mind off how rotten you're feeling.

Finally, do tell your friends and family that you aren't feeling great; that way if you snap at them, they'll understand and forgive you.

I'm always here if you have any more questions. And remember, be kind to yourself.

Take care,

Clover XXX

After reading over the letter, Clover says, "It's almost perfect. I'm just going to add one thing." She deletes "Take care, Clover XXX" and replaces it with "Take care, Clover and Amy* (*Amy is my niece and cowriter of the agony aunt pages)."

I stare at her. "You can't do that. What will you tell Saffy?"

"The truth: that you're giving me a highly valuable thirteen-year-old's perspective. As long as she doesn't have to cough up any more spondulicks, she won't mind."

"Thanks, Clover." I grin at her, delighted. (Wait till Sophie and the D4 gang in school spot my name in their fave mag. Yowsers! They'll be seaweed green.) "But shouldn't it go alphabetically? Amy and Clover."

"Don't push it." She nudges me with her shoulder.

"Hiya, girls," Martie says as she bounces into the room. "Have you seen Prue? I promised to have a look at the blender for her. It's not working and she wants to make hummus for the babies."

I wrinkle my nose. Hummus? There's no way Alex will eat hummus, and Evie only eats baby food.

"I think she's upstairs," Clover says. "Martie?"

Martie is staring at Clover's screen saver: Matt Munroe in all his topless glory, eyes blazing emerald green with a fleck of blue just under the iris of his right eye.

"That's Matt Munroe," Clover says. "Gorgeous, isn't he? In fact, I'm interviewing him in Miami. Amy's coming too. We're flying out tomorrow."

Martie's still rooted to the spot.

"Are you all right, Martie?" I ask. "You look as if you've seen a ghost."

She tears her gaze away from the computer. "I have to . . . um . . . do something . . . in the garden, I think . . . or the kitchen."

"I thought you were looking for Prue?" I say. "She's upstairs."

"Prue? Ah, yes, Prue. Thanks for reminding me, Amy. See you, girls." And with that she drifts out of the room.

Clover stares after her. "He's not *that* good-looking."

I grin. "Are you kidding? And I still can't believe we're going to see him in the flesh." I squirm in my seat with excitement.

Clover smiles. "That reminds me, we're leaving first thing tomorrow — better start packing. You stay here and e-mail Seth, Beanie. Give me a yell when you're finished. I need to heap love on Brains." (He left on Sunday morning, and I know she's missing him.)

Once Clover has skipped out of the room, I sit at the desk for a few minutes, thinking about Seth. I still haven't told Clover what happened; I haven't had a chance. Besides, I don't really want to talk about it, even with her.

I know Seth and I aren't together anymore, but I really, really want to tell him my news. I know he'll be excited for me — he's never been to America, and he's obsessed with New York. But I can hardly contact him now, though, can I? Not after what I said — which, to be honest, I'm starting to seriously regret.

I shuffle uncomfortably. I'm sure he's too busy to check his e-mail; Jin's lithe limbs are probably cling-wrapped to his tanned torso right this second. If he wasn't already with her, I'm sure I must've driven him straight into her arms. Maybe they're kissing. My back stiffens. They'd better not be, even if we have broken up.

My fingers are itching to type. What the heck! I'll just do it.

Dear Seth,
    I know we're not together anymore, and maybe you're not too interested in hearing from me at the moment, but I thought you'd like to know that I'm off to Miami, Florida, U.S. of A-mazing, tomorrow!!!
    Can you believe it?

Lil' old *moi*!

I nearly dropped dead when Mum said yes. I still can't quite get my head around it.

Here's what happened. . . . This journo on Clover's mag was supposed to be interviewing Matt Munroe, but she hurt herself, so Clover's taking over. Clover managed to change her first-class ticket for two normal ones, and I'm going to share her hotel room, so it won't cost a thing. Isn't she a doll?

Miami, here I come.

I'll tell you all about it when I get back. Don't be too jealous — at least you have sun over there in Pastaville.

Toodle-pip — or should I say, *Hasta luego,* baby!

And sorry for forgetting to say happy birthday the other day (I hadn't forgotten, honestly!), and sorry for all that other business on the phone and everything. I hope you don't hate me.

Best,

Amy

"Amy?"

I whip around. Kit's standing behind me. Clicking

off my Hotmail account, I swing around on the chair.

"Sorry to disturb you," he says, "but there was no one in the kitchen. Jack got into one of the bins. He was trying to eat a nappy when I caught him. I cleaned it all up and put a brick on top of the bin to stop him doing it again. Tell yer mam to replace the brick every time she uses the bin."

I laugh. "Eating a nappy? Yuck! I'll tell her, no problem."

Kit looks over my shoulder. "Who's that?" he asks, pointing at the screen saver. "He looks familiar."

"Matt Munroe. Big Hollywood film star. Actually, I'm flying to Miami tomorrow to interview him with Clover."

He whistles. "Didn't know you were a journalist. Impressive."

"I'm not really. I just help Clover out sometimes. She works for a magazine in Dublin."

"Miami, eh? I'm jealous. Travel safe." He smiles at me, and I melt inside.

Matt Munroe, eat your heart out.

♥ Chapter 28

And how does Mills feel about the imminent arrival of her very best friend in the whole stratosphere? Is she leaping around the place with excitement? I have no idea. You see, we're going to surprise her. Ria and Rex Costigan (Mum says they used to be plain old Rita and Ron before they became such big shots in the movie world) are in on it too. Clover has sworn them to secrecy.

Ria was the one who finalized the interview details with Clover over the phone. She also promised Mum she'd keep an eye on me; otherwise Mum would never have let me go.

At first, Ria wasn't convinced that Clover should be doing the *Goss* interview at all (she obviously remembers Clover's babysitting incident vividly), but

Saffy managed to convince her that, although Clover may not be all that reliable with children, she *is* one of Ireland's most talented young journalists.

You should see Clover's face as she repeats what Saffy said—for the third time—while we're on the plane to Heathrow. It's as if she's floating on air. (Technically speaking, I suppose she is!)

"Saffy thinks I'm talented, Beanie. Isn't that cool?"

"Clover, you're seventeen and you're writing for a national magazine. Of course you're talented."

"We writers need a lot of encouragement," she says dreamily. "We have very low self-esteem. It comes from all the rejection."

I stifle a snort. Clover and low self-esteem don't belong in the same airplane, let alone the same sentence. And rejection? Ha! When was the last time Clover was rejected?

We're flying over the Irish Sea, toward Heathrow, and Mills still has no idea that we'll be standing on her doorstep in, oh, about twelve hours' time—although, they're five hours behind the U.K. in Miami, so we'll actually see her in seven hours. I explain this to Clover, but her eyes just glaze over.

"Wake me up after the geography lecture," she says, yawning. "I'm taking a nap."

Clover isn't a huge fan of flying. She gripped my hand tightly as we took off. Luckily, the flight to London is short and there hasn't been much turbulence, so she's settled down now.

She clicks her seat back without checking behind her first, and there's a *CRUNCH*, followed by a loud "Ow!"

She turns around to beam at the male passenger in the seat behind, who is clutching his knees. "So sorry," she says, fluttering her eyelashes.

He softens up and smiles back. "No problem."

Clover could get away with murder.

The air above Heathrow is buzzing with planes waiting to land, and we have to circle twice before descending.

Clover stares out of the window anxiously. "We're very close to that Ryanair plane. I hate this bit. I wish he'd just get on with it and land."

"*She*," I say. "The pilot's a woman. Weren't you listening to the safety messages?"

"'Course not; I was reading my mag." She stares at me. "*Siúcra*, I wish you hadn't told me that."

"Why?"

"Men are much safer pilots."

"Clover! Do you really believe that?"

She nods and then gulps as we drop a little in the air. "See?" she says, her knuckles white from clutching the armrest.

"That was just a pocket of low air pressure," I reassure her. "There's nothing wrong with women pilots. They'd hardly be flying planes if they weren't qualified. Women drivers are far safer than male ones; that's a scientific fact. I bet it's the same with pilots. You're being very sexist, Clover, and it's not like you."

"I know, I know, but when it comes to flying, I'm not logical."

We drop again and she gasps and screws her eyes shut. I hold her hand and squeeze. "Nearly there."

If she's this bad on a short hop to London, what will she be like on the nine-hour flight to Miami? I'm starting to feel nervous myself.

We land safely in London. Clover is mightily relieved and crumples in her seat as soon as we come to a standstill beside the terminal building, as if she's a puppet and someone's just let go of her strings. "Phew," she says, letting out a long, snaking sigh. "One flight down, one to go."

I don't want to point out that it's actually one down, *three* to go — the return flights.

We join the queue for the exit. The air inside the

plane is warm and smells of sweaty bodies and curry, and I'm relieved when we thank the air stewards and step outside into fresh oxygen.

"You're always herded around like cattle in airports," Clover grumbles as we walk down the curved corridor to transfer onto the Miami flight. "It's so undignified."

We've only taken carry-on luggage, so we walk straight past the shuddering, lumbering baggage carousels and catch a packed bus to Terminal 3.

"This is more like it," Clover says as we walk into the super-smart shopping area. She pulls me into the Gucci shop, where she tries on some sunglasses: huge Jackie O ones that cover most of her upper face. Putting one hand under her chin and the other on her hip, she purses her lips and vogues. "Do I look fabulous?"

"Utterly, darling," I say, laughing. I try on an equally huge pair and check myself out in the mirror. I look ridiculous. I put them back on the rack and then glance at my watch. "Shouldn't we go to the gate?"

"Nah." Clover picks up another pair of glasses. "This is far more fun than waiting in a big sweaty old holding pen. We have at least an hour to kill."

"Are you sure? The ticket says boarding closes at ten thirty."

"But they mean eleven." She waves her hand at me dismissively. "Don't worry, we have loads of time."

We try on ultra-expensive Burberry coats — Clover, a short black mac; me, a beige trench coat. Clover looks amazingly glam; I look like a dodgy private detective. Then we wash our hands in the special basin in the Jo Malone shop and test some of the perfumes.

Clover sprays so much Orange Blossom on her neck that she has a coughing fit, her eyes streaming. She even splutters over the shop assistant. The woman doesn't seem to mind, though; she just smiles at Clover and hands her a tissue.

Clover wipes some of the perfume off. "Don't want to suffocate my fellow passengers on the flight. Speaking of which, what time is it, Beanie?"

"Ten forty! Clover, we need to run. The gate's fifteen minutes' walk from here, and we have to go through the metal detector things again."

Clover pales. "But we've been through security. Back in Dublin."

"Yes, but we have to go through it again. Mum was quite specific about it; she said to be sure to leave enough time. After 9/11 they're very thorough. Especially for the States."

Clover frowns. "You know what that means, Beanie? Run!"

We weave through the crowds with a lot of "Excuse me's" and get to the security area in record time. Clover whips off her sky-blue Juicy hoodie and hands it to me, so she's left wearing just a skimpy tank top, and before I can say anything, she has dashed up to a ruddy-faced security guard in his twenties. (Clover has charming security guards down to a T.)

"We're going to miss our flight," she says dramatically, fluttering her hand over her barely covered and by now heaving chest. "Can you help us? Please?" She bats her eyelashes at him.

"No problem, love. This way, please."

He escorts us into the Strictly Flight Staff Only area, where a gray-haired man is standing by the metal-detector. "Damsels in distress, Duncan?" he says to his colleague with a wink.

Duncan grins and his face goes even redder.

"Thank you so much, Dunc," Clover coos, touching his arm. "We're so grateful. You're a doll."

He blushes even deeper and stammers, "I'll ring the gate . . . let them know you're . . . on your way."

"You are a sweetie," Clover says with a smile. "It's Gate 8. Clover Wildgust and Amy Green. I won't forget this."

We sprint to the gate. A single air hostess is standing behind the desk, running her fire-engine-red nails impatiently over her collection of torn-off ticket stubs. A huge American Airlines plane is framed in the window behind her.

"Clover Wildgust and Amy Green?" she says, glaring at us. She is not a happy camper.

We both nod furiously.

"You are the last to board the plane. By a long stretch. Count yourselves very lucky."

"Yes. Thanks." I thrust my passport and ticket at her. She examines my horrible convict-like photo, tears off my ticket stub, and hands everything back to me without comment.

Clover looks stunning in her passport photo. She had it taken professionally, at great expense — and even the air hostess is impressed.

"Nice pic," she says resentfully.

The plane is ginormous; there must be at least three hundred people squeezed into it. It's divided into sections. As we walk past the very swish first-class seats, Clover gives a dramatic sigh. "See what I gave up for you, Bean Machine? Nine hours of sheer luxury. You press a button and they turn into beds."

In economy, Clover asks, "What seat are you in, Beanie?"

"32A."

She chuckles. "Didn't know they did it by bra size."

"Ha bloody ha," I say. "I suppose you're in 38DD, then?"

She studies her ticket. "Hang on a sec. They must have made a mistake. I'm in 36F. That can't be right. We have to sit together. I can't fly for nine hours on my own. I'll crack up." She starts to look very agitated.

"Please take your seats, ladies," an orange-faced air steward says. (I try not to stare at the giveaway fake tan marks on the sides of his hands.)

"But we have to sit *together*!" Clover practically screeches.

I explain the problem to the steward, and he smiles. "I'll sort it out; don't you worry. Nervous flyer, is she?"

"Very."

In the end, a large German man agrees to swap seats with me. He doesn't mind at all; he gets my aisle seat.

After shuffling along the middle aisle, Clover and

I sit down. There's a small TV screen in the back of the headrests of the seats in front and pink blankets in plastic bags on our seats.

Clover takes the eye mask out of the welcome pack and pulls it down over her forehead.

"Very Holly Golightly in *Breakfast at Tiffany's*," I say.

"Clever you." Clover smiles. "I do love that film. Audrey Hepburn and that cute blond writer. And the cat called Cat."

"I know. You gave it to me for Christmas last year."

"Did I? Clever me, in that case. Now, let's see what movie we're going to watch first." She pulls the in-flight magazine out of the pouch in front of her and flicks to the film listings.

"*We?*" I ask.

"Yes, we, Beanie. It won't be much fun watching a film on my own. I need someone to poke when it gets to the good bits."

I grin. "As long as it has Johnny Depp in it, I don't mind."

"Even better"—Clover points at the magazine—"look, *Just Add Water*, starring the one and only Matt Munroe. It doesn't come out in Dublin for another month. Cool! Useful for the interview too."

We read the blurb. Matt is playing a surfer in love with a mermaid who teaches him the secrets of the sea. According to the review, he spends most of the film in surfing shorts — what's not to like?

"I thought that flight would never end." Clover lets go of my hand, which she has been clutching for the last twenty minutes, and stretches. Clover lasted two films before nodding off and snoring her way across the Atlantic. She woke up just in time to clutch my hand during landing. I flex my fingers a few times; Clover has quite a grip.

We've just landed at Miami International Airport, and the sun is splitting the heavens — yeah! There's a heat shimmer on the runway.

I smile to myself. Miami! I'm in Miami!

♥ Chapter 29

The movie company has sent a car to collect us—a huge gleaming tar-black limousine with leather seats and enough room inside to play hockey. The driver, a tanned man in a white short-sleeved shirt and navy tie, opens the passenger door for us.

"I could get used to this," Clover says.

Miami is insanely hot, and the car's deliciously cool air-conditioning is like icy fingers running up and down my skin. I relax against the seat and stare out the window as we pull away.

"How far are we from the city?" Clover asks the driver.

"Thirty minutes' drive, ma'am, depending on the traffic," the driver replies politely.

We settle back to enjoy the ride — and that's when we both see it: our first palm tree. Tall and willowy and so very Miami. Clover grins at me, and I nod and grin back.

We power along the highway, drinking in all the sights: the huge wide roads, the rhino-size cars and SUVs, and the squat red hacienda-style houses with dark-pink flowers spilling over the walls.

As we get closer to the city, there are long-stretching suburbs of squat single-story shopping malls, complete with all kinds of small shops. Their names crack me and Clover up — Patty's House of Curl Up and Dye, Citizen Canine Pet Store, Leaven and Earth Bakery.

Soon we're driving past glam modern houses with acres of tinted glass and lush green gardens until, finally, there it is: the sea, sparkling and shimmering in front of us like a giant oasis.

We're still smiling insanely as we pull up at the hotel, a steel and glass skyscraper overlooking the bay.

"Twin Palms Hotel, ladies," the driver announces.

We walk through the doors, into the super-cold lobby, and blink several times, our eyes adjusting to the murky darkness. The reception desk is manned by a team of black-suited men and women in their twenties; all are insanely good-looking.

Clover gives a low whistle. "Fancy schmancy."
Then, not in the least bit intimidated, she strides
toward the desk and smiles at one of the men. "Clover
Wildgust," she says. "Checking in. The room was
booked by Uptown Pictures."

The man clicks away on the keyboard in front of
him, then says, "I'm afraid there's a slight problem
with your room, Ms. Wildgust."

My heart sinks. I knew it was all too good to be
true: there's no room booked, and we'll have to camp
out on the beach.

"We're fully booked this week," the receptionist
continues, "so we've had to upgrade you to a suite."

Clover grins at him. "That'll be just fine and
dandy. *Dia duit, a chairde.*"

He stares at her. "Excuse me?"

"It's Irish for 'Thanks.'"

His eyes light up. "You speak Gaelic? How darling. Rhonda, Tibby, this girl speaks Gaelic."

Two women scuttle toward him and smile at
Clover.

"Say something else," he says. "It's so precious."

"*Póg mo —*"

"*Tá Miami go deas,*" I cut in. Clover's Irish is hope-
less, and she was about to say something rather rude.
"That means 'Miami is beautiful.'"

"An bhfuil cead agam dul go dtí an leithreas?" Clover says, determined not to be outdone — that actually means "Can I go to the toilet, please?" (It's one of the first Irish phrases you learn when you're in preschool.)

I giggle.

"Oh, that's awesome, honey," one of the women says. "My great-grandmother was from County Clare. I wish I could speak Gaelic."

"Actually, we call it Irish in Ireland," I explain. "Gaelic means Irish in the Irish language, if you know what I mean."

"Honey, whatever you call it, it sounds just darling. You need anything, you just ask for Tibby, ya hear?"

In the lift on the way up to our suite, I ask Clover, "Why were you twittering on in Irish?"

"You heard Tibby. If we want anything, we just have to ask. There is method to my madness, Beanie. You have to play to your strengths, and in America, being Irish is one of them."

Our room, the South Beach Suite, is jaw-droppingly amazing.

"Wow!" Clover squeals, opening the door and then standing back to let me in.

"Double wow!" I scan the room, taking in the huge plate-glass windows overlooking the sea; the white silk curtains, complete with enough floaty voile to make dozens of bridal veils; the swish glass writing desk, with matching chair; the two white leather sofas; and the giant brushed-steel fruit bowl, groaning with fruit.

There's a door to the left.

I open it and step into the bedroom, my eyes taking in its vast super-king-size bed and view of the swanky hotel swimming pool.

The door to the bathroom is open. Creamy marble from floor to ceiling. A bath the size of Clover's Mini Cooper and a walk-in shower with several space-age silver shower nozzles.

Clover flops down on the bed, and the plump feather duvet gives a gentle whispery *phew* under her body. "I could get *so* used to this," she purrs.

♥ Chapter 30

We're standing on the doorstep of the Costigans' rented house. Like everything else in Miami, the house is supersized. As we hike up the huge white marble steps to the front door, a plump green lizard as big as a mouse scuttles in front of our feet, making us jump.

Clover gives a squeal and curls her toes up in her flip-flops. "Gross." She flaps her hands in the air and pushes me forward, as if I'm her human reptile shield. "I hate those things."

The lizard stops for a split second, as if it's checking me out, then scurries off into the shrubbery.

I watch it go and smile. "It's not going to hurt you."

"You don't know that. Maybe they bite."

"They don't bite," someone says.

We look up. Marlon is standing in the doorway, wearing a navy baseball cap, white surfing shorts, and a light-blue Abercrombie T-shirt. His hair is blonder than I remember.

"Hi, Clover," he says, his eyes fizzing like sparklers. "Remember me?"

"How could I forget?" Clover grins at him. "How's Godfather Louis?"

. "Good. He sent me a hundred euros for my birthday."

Clover whistles. "Did he, now? Lucky old you."

"I could take you out to dinner, if you like, seeing as I'm flush." *Ping!* His ears turn bright pink.

"That's very sweet of you," says Clover, "but I couldn't possibly eat up all your birthday money like that. And I don't think my boyfriend would like it. He's the jealous type."

Marlon's face falls. "Oh."

"But you can buy me an ice cream or something. How about that?"

"Deal." He's staring at her with a big goofy smile on his face. He really is besotted.

Clover must be used to boys gazing at her like that, because she doesn't seem to notice.

"Where's Mills?" I ask him.

"Downstairs, reading Betty a story. She's putting her to bed tonight; Mum and Dad are out. They say hi. Mum's going to take you both to the interview tomorrow. She'll collect you at ten at your hotel. Message delivered. And now, welcome to our humble abode." Marlon steps back, sweeping his hand in front of him, as if he's conducting an orchestra. "Please come in."

"He's such a freaky little dude," Clover whispers as we walk up the steps and into the — you guessed it — massive two-story living room. The floor is made of white marble, the walls are stark white, and there's a swirling red-and-orange abstract painting, as big as the side of a bus, on the wall facing us. A giant red glass chandelier drips from the ceiling. "Wow, wow, wow!" says Clover. "What a place!"

"Wait till you see the swimming pool," Marlon says. "Did you bring your bikini? Or you could always go topless . . ." He has a funny look on his face, and his ears are pinking up again.

I wrinkle my nose. "Marlon!"

Clover just laughs. "You wish, freakoid."

"Who's that, Marlon?" Mills shouts up the stairs.

"Just the pool boy," Marlon lies easily. "He's gone now."

"Oh, OK. Betty won't go to sleep. Can you find

her *Barbie Ballet Dreams* DVD? We're coming up to watch it."

Clover pulls me through a doorway and into the kitchen. It's like something out of a magazine — and so clean! Not a toast crumb in sight. "Quick! Hide," she says.

I pull open what looks like a cupboard, but it turns out to be a fridge. "Oops." I laugh.

"She's coming," Marlon hisses.

Clover and I run behind the door, and I press my hand over my mouth to stop my giggles.

"I think I heard a noise in the kitchen," I hear Marlon say.

"What kind of noise?" Mills asks from the other side of the door.

"Dunno. You'd better check it out."

Mills walks cautiously into the kitchen, Betty trailing behind her.

"Now!" Clover whispers.

We jump out and yell, "Surprise!"

Mills gasps and jumps at least six inches in the air while Betty starts screaming and Marlon bursts into manic and very girlie giggles.

"Talk about giving me a heart attack," Mills says. She looks completely shocked. "What are *you* doing here?"

"Clover's interviewing Matt Munroe for the *Goss*," I explain. "We just arrived. The Costigans know all about it. We swore them to secrecy."

Mills beams. "This is *sooooo* cool. I'm *sooooo* pleased to see you." She gives me a tight hug, almost crushing my ribs.

"Easy, tiger," I say.

"Sorry." She lets go of me, but she can't stop smiling. "I just can't believe you're really here. This is so cool. How long are you staying?"

"Only three days, unfortunately."

We're interrupted by Betty, who is still sobbing.

"Hush, Betty," Mills says gently. "You know Clover, and this is my friend Amy. Don't be scared."

She's clutching Mills's leg, her lower lip wobbling.

"You should have seen your face, Betty," Marlon says. "Aaagh!" He makes an exaggerated horror-movie face and laughs. "You're such a scaredy-cat."

Mills wipes Betty's tears away with her fingers. "Let's find your Barbie movie."

Finally, after two chocolate bars, a heaping bowl of warm microwaved popcorn, and half a Barbie movie, Betty's eyes start to droop, and Mills lifts her down to bed.

Clover gives Marlon ten dollars to skedaddle. He bargains her up to fifteen, then toddles off to play Xbox in his room. We're alone at last.

"So let's get down to business, Mills," Clover says when Mills comes back from putting Betty to bed. "Most important, have you met Matt Munroe yet? What's he like? Is he as dreamy as he looks on screen?"

"More," Mills says. "He looks much better in the flesh."

"How much flesh have you seen, exactly?" I ask.

Mills blushes. "Quite a lot, actually. He and Ed are always using the pool."

"Hang on a minute," I say, "you mean the Matt you were talking about in your e-mails is Matt *Munroe*?"

"Of course," Mills says. "Who did you think I meant?"

Clover stares at Mills. "Let's get this straight. You've been hanging out with Matt Munroe?"

"Yes. And his friend Ed."

Clover hits her head with her hand. "*Siúcra ducra*, I should have been a better babysitter. We'd probably be the hottest couple in Hollywood by now . . . photos in all the magazines." Her eyes twinkle.

"Clover!" I say, giving her a look. She's read Mills's e-mails. She knows how Mills feels about him.

Clover looks sheepish. "Sorry, Mills. I was getting a bit carried away there."

Mills shrugs. "It's OK. I was a bit like that too when I first met him. It wears off."

"Really?" I ask. "You don't like him anymore?"

"I do. But Ed's fun too, in a different way. He seems more like the boys back home; he loves kidding around and making everyone laugh. Matt's only sixteen, but he's very mature. I find it hard to talk to him sometimes. But *of course,* I still like him. I've seen those pecs up close and personal, remember?"

"So which is it to be?" I ask. "Matt or Ed?"

Mills clicks her tongue. "I can't decide. I think I like them both. Matt, well, Matt's Matt — what can I say?" She shrugs. "But Ed's cute too. But he's a bit immature compared with Matt. He's always splashing me in the pool and throwing lumps of ice down my back. Things like that."

"So many boys," Clover quips, "so little time. But, hey, if Ed's throwing ice at you, he definitely likes you."

"You think?"

"One hundred percent."

Mills smiles. "Wait till you meet Matt. Then you'll see my dilemma." She closes her eyes and sighs dreamily.

I snort loudly. "Mills! I think the heat's getting to you."

"You just wait, Amy Green," she says, opening her eyes. "Matt Munroe will make even *you* melt, Miss Ice Queen. I guarantee it."

♥ Chapter 31

On Friday morning I wake up at four a.m., five a.m., and again at six twenty a.m. At six forty I finally creep out of bed. I've been lying ramrod straight, trying not to toss around and wake Clover—but if I have to lie still any longer I'll go crazy. My watch may read six forty, but my body clock is saying, "Get up, girl; it's nearly noon and I want to explore Miami. You're wasting precious U.S. of A-mazing time!"

I was so exhausted last night that I didn't even hear Clover snoring and fell asleep as soon as my jet-lagged head hit the pillow.

We hung out with Mills at the Costigans' place for as long as I could stay awake. Clover insisted on having a dip in the pool in her bra and knickers—until

Mills caught Marlon spying on her and taking snaps with his mobile.

Creeping out of the bedroom, I spot Clover's copy of the *Goss* lying on the floor. I pick it up and head for the balcony. The sun is already up, playing hopscotch on the turquoise water, which stretches out as far as I can see. The palm trees on the hotel's grounds sway gently in the early morning breeze. Just offshore there's a series of small, sandy islands; you could easily swim out to them. Hundreds of expensive-looking white and navy yachts are moored at the marina, their tall masts soaring up into the clear blue sky. It's stunning, and even this early it's already warm.

I sit on the lounger and open the magazine to the Efa interview. Clover wanted me to wait to read it until it was printed in the *Goss* and properly laid out with photographs. She picked up a copy, hot off the press, at Cork Airport, and I've had a quick look but haven't had the chance to fully read it until now.

Ireland's Hottest New Star — Efa Valentine
Exclusive interview by Clover M. Wildgust

Efa Valentine, 17, is best known for her recent Oscar-nominated role as Joan of Arc. I caught up with her in her native Cork.

Efa has been acting for most of her life. She landed her first role at the tender age of six, when she played Colin Firth's stepdaughter in *Miracle Walk*.

"I went to a drama school on Saturday mornings," Efa explains, "and an Irish casting agent, Rex Costigan, spotted me — that led to my first film."

Like any ordinary teenager, Efa goes to school — Bandon Grammar — and is taking her Leaving Certificate next year. During filming she has a tutor. "Big exams next year, all right." She groans. "But I want to go to college, in case the acting doesn't work out. I'd like to study English at Trinity College, I think. Or maybe history."

When she's at home, Efa keeps fit by running with her rescue dog, Miley. She keeps in touch with her friends when she's filming abroad, but she doesn't find being miles from home easy. "My friends are really supportive," she says. "But when I'm away I miss things — birthdays, parties, that kind of thing."

And has she encountered any jealousy? "Not really. My friends are pretty cool about everything. They slag me all the time about the awards and stuff. They're always asking me about my costars too. If I'm doing a film with a boy, it's always, 'Did you kiss him, Efa?'"

And does she? Kiss her costars, I mean. She laughs. "No way! On a film set you'd never get a chance — there'd always be someone watching. And after filming, I'm so wrecked I just fall straight into bed."

But what about back home? Anyone special? "I wish," she says with a grin. "Any cuties out there, please apply. Seriously, though, at the moment I'm just having fun hanging out with my friends."

Efa was delighted by her Oscar nomination. "It's about time we Irish girls started to make a splash in Hollywood. And I had a ball at the Oscars. I even got to keep the Chanel dress I wore — yeah!"

After a hectic year, Efa's currently reading a couple of possible scripts and catching up with her friends. But watch out, Hollywood: Efa Valentine's here to stay!

"Morning, sunshine." Clover grins at me and rubs her eyes. "You're up early. It's not even seven." She looks down at the magazine pages. "What do you think?"

"It's brilliant, Clover. Really professional. And you got in the question about boyfriends."

"I certainly did. Thanks to you, Beanie." She smiles. "I'm pleased with it all right. And the pics look great, don't they? That red Oscar dress is really something." Her stomach rumbles loudly. "I'm starving. Let's have brekkie. Pull on some clothes, Beans;

we can grab a shower later. How's the stomach? Any period cramps?"

"No, I'm OK."

"Good, then let's mush, husky."

Even the breakfast is spectacular. Clover has an omelet specially cooked for her by a cute guy in a sparkling white chef's outfit. I think she only said "Yes, please" because he was so attractive; she only picks at it. She also has a large bowl of fruit and a chocolate muffin.

I devour two heaping bowls of the sweetest and juiciest watermelon I've ever tasted, some scrambled eggs, a sausage (not as tasty as an Irish sausage, but nice all the same), two slices of Swiss cheese, and a pastry thing with apricot jam and a rich dark-yellow custard in the middle. I feel like the Very Hungry Caterpillar, eating and eating and eating until I practically burst.

"We'd better skip lunch or we'll go back looking like Heffalumps," Clover says, rubbing her stomach and sipping her latte slowly. She likes the *idea* of coffee more than the actual coffee itself — she thinks it makes her look sophisticated.

At twenty past ten, we're still sitting on a red leather sofa in the lobby, waiting for Ria. Clover is rereading her Matt Munroe notes. She's getting a little obsessive now — she practically knows them all by heart.

We hear a loud *parp-parp* outside and look through the window. Ria is waving from a sleek gray convertible Mercedes.

Clover grins. "That's our ride, Beanie."

I climb into the back, and Clover sits beside Ria.

"Sorry I'm late, girls," Ria says. Her hair is beach-babe blond and her makeup is perfect. "Betty was a bit clingy this morning. So how was your flight? Good? And the hotel? It's rather plush, isn't it? And I hear they gave you a suite. How cool is that?" (She doesn't bother waiting for an answer to any of her questions before plowing on.) "Now, Clover, I know you're a bit of a novice at this interviewing malarkey, but don't worry, you'll be fine. You have plenty of notes, I see" — she nods at Clover's blue folder — "so you'll only need a few quotes to bung into the piece and make it interesting for your teen audience . . . which is just as well, as they've cut your interview time down to ten minutes."

Clover looks aghast. "Ten minutes? But I was promised thirty. I'll never get all my questions asked in ten minutes."

Ria smiles at her. "You'll be fine. Ask the most important ones first, and then just keep the questions rolling. They may give you some extra time, if you're lucky."

I check out Clover's face in the rearview mirror. She's not happy. She catches my eye and raises her eyebrows. I hope we have time to carry out our carefully hatched plan.

"Here we are," Ria announces, pulling up outside a huge hotel. "The Coconut Grove Plaza. Uptown Pictures has hired a suite for the interviews. I'll introduce you to Matt's people, and then I'll buzz off, if you don't mind. I have urgent e-mails coming out of my ears. Everyone wants a piece of me, like yesterday." She yawns. "I'm utterly wiped."

The hotel is bright and glossy, and a little bit tacky, with lots of shiny black marble and loads of chrome fittings. There are lamps in the shape of coconut trees, and in the immense lobby, a waterfall splashes from one of the walls. It is lit from underneath by pink lights in the shape of flamingos.

"Tasteful," Clover says, nudging me in the ribs.

I giggle.

"Clover and Amy, this is Vim Kruger," Ria says, introducing us to a woman holding a clipboard. "She's the publicist for Uptown Pictures. I'll leave you in her capable hands."

Vim looks scary. Her dark-brown bob has a razor-sharp fringe, and she's wearing a tailored black suit, black fishnet tights, and black pumps.

"Nice to meet you." She throws out her hand and grasps the tips of Clover's fingers in a very odd handshake, before giving me a funny look and then pretty much ignoring me. She obviously doesn't think I'm very important. She looks down at her clipboard. "You must be from the London *Times*."

"No," Clover says. "The *Goss* magazine."

Vim squints at her clipboard, runs a long pointy red nail down the list, and then stops. "Found you." She puts a neat checkmark beside both our names. "If you'll just take a seat in the restaurant"— she nods toward a door to the right —"I'll call you in about twenty minutes. Matt's with *Chicago People* at the moment, followed by *Movie Emporium*; then you'll be up." She tilts her head at Clover, ignoring me again. "OK?"

"Yes. Thank you," Clover says calmly, as if she does movie-star interviews every day of her life.

We sit down in the restaurant and look around. There are dozens of men and women barking into mobiles, tapping on laptops, and playing with Black-Berrys. They all look ultra busy and organized.

Clover starts to look nervous. "I'm way out of my

depth here, Beanie. What was I thinking? I can't do this." She makes as if to get up.

I push her down with my arm. "You'll be fine. You have all your questions prepared, and I bet half of these people have never even watched a Matt Munroe film. They're far too old. Matt is going to love your questions. And besides, there's no way anyone else knows about the Irish connection."

At breakfast earlier, we went over our plan. Kit had called into Haven House just before we left for the airport to say he'd remembered where he'd seen Matt Munroe before. I haven't said anything to Mills yet, just in case Kit has it wrong — but if he is right, our information is Hollywood dynamite.

"I'm not sure I'll go there, Beanie. I think I'll just play it straight. I don't want to get thrown out or anything," Clover says nervously. "There must be a reason he doesn't talk about his Irish background."

"Don't you dare chicken out! It's breaking news, Clover. Saffy will be so impressed. You have to be brave — what's the worst that can happen?"

"*She* might just kill me with her razor talons." Clover points at Vim, who is tottering toward us.

"You're up, *Goss*," she says. "*Movie Emporium* is late. They'll have to slot in after you."

We follow Vim into a lift at the side of the lobby;

she operates the controls with a key. "Now, remember, ten minutes, OK?" she says. "His agent will be in there with him. And you've studied the list of recommended questions, yes?"

The lift door pings open and she hustles us out. "The Flamingo Suite. Knock once and then wait."

The lift door pings closed again and she's gone.

"Recommended questions?" Clover looks at me, baffled.

I shrug.

As we head down the corridor, a door at the end opens and a middle-aged man in a cream linen suit walks out. He's stuffing a Dictaphone into his briefcase. "You here for Matt?" he asks us.

We nod.

"Good luck. You won't get much past his agent. Pity — Matt seems nice."

Clover grabs my arm. "I can't do this."

"Yes, you can. I'll be with you, Clover. And I think we should play up our Irishness. Complete with your five-year-old's grasp of our native tongue. See if Matt bites. Agreed?"

"Great idea, Beanie. But we only have ten minutes, remember."

I push Clover though the door. And there he is, standing in the hallway of the suite, ready to greet us — Matt Munroe, in person! I instantly go pink and completely forget our plan. Mills was right; he's even better-looking in real life. I want to reach out and touch his tanned cheek, but I stop myself. He smells gorgeous too — a fresh citrus smell, like lemons.

Clover's gawking at him as well. So much for her professionalism.

"Top o' the morning to you," I say, taking control. "I'm Amy and this is Clover. We're friends of Mills's and are here on behalf of the *Goss*. It's an Irish magazine. To be sure, to be sure." (I'm laying on the Irish blarney pretty thick.)

He looks a little taken aback but recovers quickly and says, "Hey, Amy! Great to meet ya." He grins and kisses my cheek. "Mills has told me all about you. Best buds, right?" When I get over the shock, I realize that Matt Munroe has just kissed me. I know it's only on the cheek, but my knees buckle and I almost keel over. Luckily, Clover rights me.

"Clover," she says, propping me up. "Another close friend of Mills's." She steps forward, twisting her head a little, obviously waiting for her kiss. He obliges.

Despite almost demanding her kiss, Clover is as gobsmacked as I am. We both stand there, speechless. There's an open door to the right through which

I spot a king-size bed, and I'm instantly undone. I blush even more furiously. Then Clover notices it too, and *her* cheeks start flaming. We're like a pair of lobsters.

"Who's up next?" a deep American voice calls from the bedroom.

"That's Gabe," Matt explains. "My agent. Let's see if I can get rid of him and kick back a bit. I do love the Irish brogue." He winks at me, his famous green eyes twinkling, and I melt. He doesn't seem to notice. Or else, like Clover, he's immune to adoration from the opposite sex. Maybe he thinks all girls are practically mute and have glowing pink cheeks.

"I wonder what it's like to be that good-looking?" Clover whispers as Matt talks to his agent, a tall olive-skinned man in a black polo shirt and beige trousers.

"We'll never know," I say with a shrug.

"Speak for yourself." Clover grins.

"Ladies," Gabe says, walking toward us. "You're friends of the Costigans, I believe. Great couple; really know their stuff. Still — no tricky questions, y'hear?" He grins before adding, "You got the list, right?"

"Of course," Clover says smoothly. "We'll be sticking to it rigidly."

"Great, great." He runs his hand over his bald

head. Then he turns to Matt. "I have a couple of calls to make. Back in ten, OK?"

"Can we make it longer?" Matt asks. "They've traveled all the way from Ireland." (He pronounces it *Eye-are-land*.)

"Ireland?" Gabe asks, looking at Matt nervously.

Clover nods. "A wee teen mag called the *Goss*, full of *ceol agus craic* and a wee smattering of shiny celebs. Our Irish colleens just love Matt."

Gabe smiles. "I'll talk to Vim about getting you some exclusive stills." He's obviously decided we're harmless.

"Now you're sucking diesel," Clover says with a wink.

Gabe laughs. "I have no idea what you're saying, but I'll see what I can do."

As soon as he's gone, Matt leads us to some swish leather armchairs and we sit down. "Can I get you guys a drink?" he asks politely, hovering behind Clover's chair.

"No, we're fine, thanks," Clover says. Her folder is open on her knees and she's setting up the Dictaphone on the coffee table in front of her.

"How's Mills?" he asks. "Things have been kinda hectic. We haven't been over for a few days. But it's tough keeping Ed away." He beams.

"Ah," Clover says. "Thought so. Your friend has a bit of a crush, does he?"

Matt just keeps smiling. "I couldn't possibly say."

"And what do you think of Irish girls yourself?" Clover asks. "Our readers are dying to know."

Matt laughs. "You cut to the chase, don't ya? If Gabe were here, he'd tell me not to answer that one. It might annoy fans in other countries. The official line is that I like girls of all nationalities, and no, I'm not seeing anyone special right now. I'm waiting for the right girl to come along. And you're supposed to be asking me about *Just Add Water*."

"Look," says Clover, "I'll come clean. I never got the recommended questions Vim and Gabe were talking about, so you're going to have to help me out here. I only have my own questions."

Matt sits down. "What kind of questions?"

She takes a deep breath. "When did you leave Ireland? Why did you change your name?"

227 ♥

♥ Chapter 32

"What?" Matt's face is ashen and his hands are shaking. "I think we'd better take this off the record." He points at the Dictaphone.

Clover reaches over and clicks it off. "Do you remember Kit Harper? From Lough Ine village in West Cork?"

Matt's eyes flicker for a second, but then he says, "No, sorry. Never heard of him. Or is it a her?"

"He remembers you, *Sean*," I say.

"What? Why did you call me that?" Matt's eyes flash and he sits up bolt straight.

"Because it's your real name. Kit said the hair and the teeth have changed, but that he'd recognize those eyes anywhere."

Matt drops his eyes to the floor and shifts around on his chair uncomfortably. "I'm sorry, you've made a mistake. I've never even been to Ireland."

I try one last time. "Strange, because Kit could have sworn it was you. He sends his regards. You used to help his mum, May, in the garden at Haven House. He does her job now. Lives on the island too."

Matt looks confused. "On his own? What about his family?"

"I'm afraid his mum died a few years ago in a boating accident. Apparently he didn't take it very well."

Matt gasps. "May's dead?"

Finally, a proper reaction! But I'm not surprised — if Matt and May were as close as Kit said they were, it must be very sad news. "Yes," I say gently. "I'm so sorry."

Matt looks genuinely distraught. "No, I'm the one who should be sorry. Lying to you like that. Ach, I'll come clean with you, girls," he says, his perfect Miami accent melting away. He has a beautiful Cork singsong lilt, tinged with Miami smoothness. "Frankly, it'll be a relief to finally talk about it. May was an amazing woman. Poor Kit; he adored her. How's he doing?"

"OK, I think. He seems to like working in the garden."

"Good. Tell him I was asking after him and that I'm sorry. May was very good to me. Kept me in pocket money for years." He sighs, blowing air out noisily, then leans back in his seat and stares off into space. "I told Gabe it was only a matter of time. People aren't stupid. Especially Cork people. And Mum hates all the lies. It was Gabe's idea. He said if I didn't go along with it, I'd have the shortest movie career in the history of Hollywood."

"Go along with what?" I ask.

He leans forward, his gaze intense. "Can I trust you both?"

We nod eagerly, dying to hear his secret.

"I'm not sixteen. I just turned twenty-one."

I gasp. And then I look at him again. The slight stubble on his cheeks, the tiny, fine crinkles around his eyes, the knowingness: of course he's not sixteen.

"My real name's Sean Whooley," he continues. "I grew up in Tragumna, near Skibbereen. My dad died when I was three. He was a fisherman. He had a heart attack when he was working, and by the time the crew got back to shore, it was too late."

"I'm sorry," I murmur.

"It's OK—I don't really remember him, to be honest. Mum worked in a hotel while I was growing up, but it closed just after I turned seventeen. She was offered a good job in Dublin, so we all moved up — me, Mum, and my brother, Ed. We lived there for a while, and then Mum met Donnie at a hoteliers' convention. He's from Miami. They did the whole long-distance thing for a while before he asked her to marry him and move over here. I was nineteen — Miami sounded cool.

"I got a job in this bar on South Beach, and that's where I met Gabe. He was sitting outside smoking a big fat cigar. He gave me his card and said to come for a screen test. I'd done some acting back in Dublin. Nothing serious — but he made it sound so attractive, I thought I'd give it another go. I had nothing to lose. So he put me forward for a few parts, but I never got anything.

"Then this high-school drama came up. They wanted a thirteen-year-old. Gabe told them I was fourteen but could play thirteen, no problem. I've always looked young for my age, and I'm pretty short, which also helped. I did the audition as a Miami teenager, and Gabe gave me a new stage name: Matt Munroe. They fell for it; I got the part, and the series became pretty popular."

"No kidding!" I say. "*West Dream High* was huge in Ireland too. But didn't your Irish friends recognize you?"

He smiles. "Sean Whooley had mousy brown hair and wore glasses. Plus, he had wonky teeth." Matt taps his teeth with his fingertip. "Veneers. And I didn't have all that many friends in Dublin, to tell the truth. I missed West Cork, so I kept myself to myself while I was in the capital. But now, it's all gotten out of hand. I spend my free time taking famous girl teenyboppers to movie premieres to raise my profile. It's horrible." He pauses. "No offense, Amy."

I smile at him. "None taken."

"I want to stop being a fake teenager and get on with my life. But what can I do? I'm stuck being Matt Munroe and hanging around with my brother, pretending he's my best friend. I like Ed, but he's so immature."

"He's fifteen!" I say, laughing.

"Exactly." Matt says. "I want to make some twenty-something friends. Go to bars, listen to bands. Get my own apartment. At the moment I have to live with Mum and Donnie and Ed. How lame is that?"

"You could come clean," Clover says. She nods at her Dictaphone. "We could help."

"Gabe would murder me. He's already signed me up for another teen movie after *Life Swap* — the one Rex is casting now. He says if the industry finds out I'm twenty-one, I'm toast."

"But Zane Danvers is in his twenties and teenagers like *him*," I point out. (Zane is the star of a hugely popular series of movies set in a performing arts school in New York.)

"For how much longer?" Matt says gloomily.

"Is that all you want to be?" I press. "A teen idol?"

He shakes his head. "Of course not. I want to do other things."

"Like what?" Clover asks.

"Don't laugh."

"We won't," I promise.

"I want to write screenplays. Comedies. When I was working as a waiter, I was writing one about an Irish waiter who falls in love with this famous American movie star but has no idea who she is. Anyway, after I met Gabe, things got a little crazy and I never finished it."

"You have to take control back," I say, "or else you'll go mad. What does your mum say?"

"She's with you. She wants me to tell the truth; she reckons I'm living a lie. Donnie says I have to decide for myself but that if I keep going another three or four years I'll earn enough to retire. He's practical that way."

"But what about *you*? Can you really live like this for another few years? Won't you crack up?" I ask.

Gabe bursts into the room. We all look up guilt-ily. "So how's the interview going, guys?" he says.

"I think I'll need a few more minutes," Clover says, waving her Dictaphone. "I forgot to switch this on."

Gabe shakes his head. "Too late for that, missy. *Movie Emporium* is outside. Use the press release; it'll be just fine, I'm sure."

"When are you guys flying back to Ireland?" Matt asks us, his Miami accent flawless again.

"Tomorrow night," I say. Is it my imagination or does he look a little panicked? Maybe he thinks we're about to divulge his secret to the international press camped downstairs.

"In that case," he says, "I'm taking you all to a res-taurant opening tonight. In South Beach. Mills too. I'll pick you up at seven. Where are you staying?"

"Twin Palms Hotel," I say.

"Matt," Gabe cuts in, "you have more interviews tomorrow, remember."

"Come on, Gabe, I need a night off."

"OK, but it's important to maintain your image," he says sternly. "Remember who you are, *Matt*."

Matt sighs. "How could I forget?"

I catch his eye and give him a gentle smile while Clover stands up. "Sounds good. He's all yours, Gabe."

As Gabe shows Clover out, Matt grabs my arm. "I need your help," he whispers urgently. "There's someone I need to —"

"Miles Gaynor, *Movie Emporium*," a tall man with square glasses bounds toward Matt, his hand out.

"See you later, Amy," Matt says, letting go of my hand and giving Miles a polite smile — one that never reaches his eyes.

"No way!" Mills squeals when we tell her Matt's story. "Betty, stop splashing your brother. Marlon, stop teasing your sister."

We're lounging beside the Costigans' pool, still reeling after our bizarre morning.

Mills turns back to us. "Twenty-one!" she whistles. "Ancient. No wonder he isn't interested in me. He's more your age, Clover."

"I think he's looking for someone even older," Clover says. "And I have Brains, remember?"

We both stare at her.

"But he's Matt Munroe," Mills points out.

"Sean Whooley, actually." Clover shrugs. "Brains is good-looking too, and at least he knows who he is. Sean's one mixed-up soldier."

"Do you think he'll come clean about his age?" I ask her.

"Doubtful. He seems to be firmly under Gabe's fat sausage finger."

"But what about the *Goss* interview?" I ask. "What are you going to write? There's nothing on your Dictaphone."

"I'll think of something, Beanie. There's always tonight. Mills, where's South Beach? Matt's taking us all to a fancy schmancy restaurant launch."

Mills's eyes goggle. "South Beach? Ha! Fabarooney! Girls, you'll love it. Dust off your best bikinis."

"Bikinis?" I ask. "For a restaurant launch?"

Mills smiles smugly. "You just wait, Amy Green."

Where have I heard that before?

♥ Chapter 33

It's 7:45 p.m. Miami time, and the best night of my life is only just getting started. I'm sitting on butter-soft white leather in the back of a spanking-new midnight-blue Rolls-Royce Phantom convertible (or "drophead," which is the correct term, according to Ed, who's a bit of a car geek). Matt's driving, and even from behind his dark Gucci shades, he's causing quite a stir: "OH, MY GOD; isn't that the guy from *West Dream High?*" "Hi, Matt, I *loooove* you! I'm your biggest fan." "Blow me a kiss, Lucas!" (His character in the show is called Lucas Luck.)

I'm wearing brand-new Jimmy Choos — also courtesy of Matt. Isn't he a sweetie? Gabe's assistant rang this very posh shop and asked for shoes for Matt's female friends, promising they'd be photographed at the red-carpet restaurant launch this evening. A girl from the shop arrived at the Costigans' place with bags and bags of shoe boxes. We had such fun trying them all on — we were like three Cinderellas.

Clover chose a pair of silver snakeskin peep-toes with dagger heels, while I went for a pair of red satin strappy sandals with kitten heels. (I didn't want to be tripping all night and making a complete fool of myself.) Mills picked pumps in a deep forest green with cute diamanté hearts on the front.

We're crawling down Ocean Drive now, the beach dipping down to the sea to our left and music pumping out into the street from the hopping bars and restaurants along the front. But none of it is as loud as our music. We have fifteen speakers (Ed has counted them), and we're singing along to "The Galway Girl," an old Irish song. It's Matt's favorite — which is kind of funny, if you think about it. He's supposed to be this big, cool movie star, and yet he listens to diddly-eye Irish ballads.

Ed has a great voice; the rest of us are just belting out what we know of the words, waving our arms in the air, clapping, and cracking up laughing.

"And I ask you, friend," Ed sings to Mills, *"what's a fella to do? 'Cause her hair was black and her eyes were blue . . ."*

Mills beams at him. Ed seems to be seriously growing on her.

There are people everywhere — walking, skating, cycling, dancing. Some of the women are in teeny tiny bikinis and heels; others are in poured-on Lycra dresses, their curvy bums doing a Marilyn Monroe–style *va-va-voom* as they walk.

We spot a bunch of teenage boys in matching shorts, runners, and pristine white tank tops, with strings and strings of what look like real pearls around their necks, worn proudly like medals at a swim meet.

Teenage girls parade up and down the strip in unzipped shorts, showing off their brightly colored bikini bottoms. Scooters nip in and out between the cars, driven by muscular boys, with long-haired girls behind, like must-have accessories, arms tightly octo-pused around the boys' waists.

The air smells of adventure: musky, tinged with expensive perfume, cigar smoke, and the tang of the sea.

And the buildings — the buildings are amazing.

Sleek, stylish Art Deco architecture and all painted in ice-cream pastels: pink, yellow, pistachio green.

We pull up for a few seconds outside a house that looks as if it's straight out of a fairy tale. It's lit up with twinkling lights, like a Christmas tree.

"One of the South Beach sights — the house where Versace was shot," Ed says, all matter-of-fact. "Killed at the gates of his own mansion. Casa Casuarina. It's a members-only club now."

"Poor guy," Clover whispers.

I shiver. It's all a bit macabre.

Matt drives on, then stops about three minutes later outside a bustling restaurant. He gets out of the car. (In his plum Prada shirt, he's definitely Matt Munroe tonight and not Sean Whooley.)

A man in a shiny navy suit runs toward him, beaming. "Mr. Munroe," he says, "we've been expecting you. I'm Tulio, manager of Café Maximus. I'll have your car parked for you immediately. If you and your guests would like to come this way . . ."

We're ushered onto a red carpet, and then *FLASH, FLASH*: I can't see a thing. Dozens of paparazzi are buzzing around Matt. Clover stumbles in her Choos. Matt seizes her arm and helps her up.

"Who's the girl? Anyone special?" a photographer demands. "What's your name, honey?"

Clover straightens her dress and composes herself. "Clover Wildgust. That's spelled W-I-L-D-G-U-S-T." She gives him her best Hollywood smile. "I'm a close friend of Matt's." She touches Matt's arm and pouts a little for the camera. She's shameless.

Mills gets in the spirit, seizing Matt's other hand. "But I'm Matt's *special* friend."

"And me," I add, cracking up and taking his elbow. "Don't forget me. I'm his *extra*-special friend."

The photographer grins. "That right, Matt? You have three girlfriends?"

Matt just laughs.

Ed is walking along behind us, looking a bit put out. I put my hand on Mills's arm. "Ed," I whisper. She nods and drops back to join him.

"So this is what it feels like to be a movie star," Clover gasps as Tulio leads us inside.

"I can see why Matt doesn't want to give it up," I say. "Must be addictive."

"If I could only learn to walk in these darned heels." She laughs, slipping again.

Later that evening Matt, Clover, and I are sitting on a low wall outside the restaurant, our backs to the beach. It's still balmy, and if you listen carefully, you can just about hear the swish of the waves over the sand. Mills and Ed have gone for a walk down the beach to "go beachcombing," according to Mills.

"Beachcombing, my posterior," Clover says with a grin, watching them stroll off together, their shoulders bumping. "Is that what they call it these days?"

"Mills loves beachcombing," I say, eager to defend my friend. "She has this thing about collecting a stone from every beach she's ever visited. She labels them with nail polish and puts them in a shoe box."

Clover snorts. "I still think they're snogging."

Matt laughs. "Snogging! That's not a word you hear in Miami. God, I miss Ireland."

"With all this?" Clover waves her arms in the air, taking in the beach and the restaurant. "I bet it's raining at home."

"Yep, but I even miss the rain. It gets so hot in Miami. Look, before I chicken out, I need to ask you both a favor." He drags a hand through his hair. "I need you to find someone for me and give them a message."

"An old girlfriend?" I ask.

He smiles at me. "You don't miss much, do you, Amy? She's probably forgotten all about me by now. But I owe her an explanation. I left Ireland without saying good-bye. It nearly broke my heart."

"You just ran away?" I ask. "But why?"

He clicks his tongue. "I wanted to travel. To have an adventure, get out of Ireland. At the time it felt so small, like one big village: claustrophobic, you know. I thought I'd meet other girls — but I haven't, not like Martie."

"What did you just say?" I ask.

"Martie. That's her name. Martina Coghill. She lives near Lough Ine. She used to know Kit Harper, so you might be able to find her through him. She got me the job with May in the first place."

No wonder Martie froze when she saw Matt's photograph. Clover is staring at me. I give her a little frown to stop her saying anything. "Don't worry," I tell Matt. "We'll help you."

An hour later, Matt is driving us back to the hotel. He's already dropped Mills and Ed off. It's past three o'clock in the morning and I can't stop yawning. Mum would have a fit if she knew I was out so late.

As we pull up outside our hotel, my phone rings. I answer it. "Hello?"

"Amy, it's Gramps. I'm in Esther's house and we asked Martie to come over urgently, just like you said. She's standing right here beside me. Now what?"

"When I say 'Now!' hand Martie your phone."

"Roger that."

"OK, Gramps — *now!*" I hand the mobile over to Matt and pray I've done the right thing. "Someone wants to talk to you," I tell him.

"Who is this?" Matt says into the phone, bemused. After a brief pause his eyes widen. "Martie, is that you? Martie." He starts to cry.

Oops, what have I done?

"Let's give him some privacy," Clover says. She opens the passenger door.

"It's a convertible, you dummy," I say. "We can still hear."

"Not if we go inside."

"Clover!" I'm dying to listen in on their conversation — but Clover's right.

We wait in the lobby, glancing out the window now and again to see if Matt's still there.

After a few minutes, Matt walks inside and hands me back the mobile.

"Well?" I say.

"Martie's pretty angry with me. But at least she didn't hang up."

"Is she coming over to see you?"

He shakes his head sadly. He looks like a puppy that's just been put outside.

"Oh." This isn't very romantic at all.

Sitting down beside us, he puts his head in his

hands. "I've really messed up this time. There'll never be another Martie. I'm such an idiot. You always know where you are with Martie. Always tells you the truth, even if you don't want to hear it." He gives a laugh. "She said my teeth look fake." He opens his mouth wide and pulls back his gums. Now he looks like a mare at a horse market. I don't want to point out that veneers *are* fake.

"Pay no attention," Clover says kindly. "They're lovely. So she knows you're Matt Munroe, but she hasn't told anyone? Or tried to contact you?"

"No." He shrugs. "That's Irish girls for you. Completely mad and stubborn as anything. Sorry, girls, no offense."

"That's OK," Clover says. "It's probably true. The stubborn bit, anyway."

Matt sighs. "I guess I'll just have to move on. Put Martie behind me. But at least I have her number now. Thanks to you two. She said I can ring her if I need to talk."

"Did she, now?" Clover looks at me, eyebrows raised.

"And will you?" I ask him.

"Every day. Until she changes her mind."

I smile: if he's that determined, there's hope yet.

♥ Chapter 34

It's hard to say good-bye to Mills. Ria has arranged for a chauffeur to bring us to the airport. Matt has a script meeting all afternoon, but Ed and Mills have come along to see us off.

"I've had such an amazing time." I grab Mills and give her a bear hug. (She smells of apples from her fruity shampoo.) "I'll miss you."

"Only two more weeks," she says. Then she whispers in my ear, "Thanks for all the advice. Ed's great. I don't know what I saw in Matt; he's far too serious for me. And good luck with Seth. I'm sorry we didn't get much time to talk, but you guys will work it out; you're made for each other."

"I hope so, Mills," I say. "I'll see you back in Dublin. Have fun with Ed. And thanks for everything."

Earlier this morning, I finally got a chance to tell Mills about what had happened with Seth and a little about Kit.

Mills said that from the way I was describing Kit, it sounded as if he and Matt were very alike — both drop-dead gorgeous, both confused.

"I think they both need to find out who they really are, Amy," she said. Mills is one smart cookie sometimes.

Talking to her made me realize just how much I miss Seth and how much he means to me. Back at the hotel, while Clover was writing up some notes for Saffy on her laptop, I went downstairs and sat down at one of the computers in the hotel's business center. I wanted to check my e-mail and was hoping there might be a message from Seth. There was!

Yowser, Amy!

Miami! You lucky thing, kiddo! It's supposed to be mega.

I'm sorry too about the phone call the other day. I was really annoyed with you afterward and frustrated that you didn't seem to believe me about Jin (as if!) — but I thought about it, and I

247 ♥

guess I was going on about her in my e-mails a lot. I missed you and maybe I wanted to make you a bit jealous. It was really childish and stupid, and I'm sorry.

I hope you don't mind, but I was so upset after our phone call that I talked to Jin about it. She said it sounded as if we were good together and worth saving and not to let you go without a fight. She said she broke up with her boyfriend once, and she missed him so much that it made her realize how much she liked him. They got back together and things are even better now.

Anyway, I hope we can work things out back in Dublin. I don't want to lose you, babe.

Love always,

Seth XXX + a million

P.S. Jin really isn't my type. Promise. I only have eyes for you!

I almost cried with relief. Jin's right: sometimes you don't realize what you've got till it's gone. I'm not going to make that mistake again.

After nearly fifteen hours of traveling, Clover and I arrive at Cork Airport on Sunday morning. I managed to get some sleep on the plane, slouched on top of Clover's shoulder, so I don't feel too bad, but Clover's in bits: she didn't sleep a wink. She rolls her head on her neck and it makes an ominous click. She scowls at me. "You were dribbling on me the whole way over the Atlantic."

"I don't dribble." I wipe the edges of my mouth with my finger. Oops, maybe I do dribble a little. I stretch over her and look out the window. Gray sky and drizzle. "Welcome back to sunny old Ireland." I sigh.

Miami, with its sun, clear blue skies, swimming pools, elephant-size SUVS, red carpets, and fancy shoes, seems like a dream.

♥ Chapter 35

Back at Haven House, Clover takes to her bed at three with jet lag. I finish up my late lunch and walk outside. Spotting a book on the patio table, I walk over. It's *Into the Wild*, the book Kit was reading in his boathouse. There's a plain white postcard sticking from between its pages, and I pull it out. To my surprise, it's a note for me.

Dear Amy,
    Sorry about the other day. Thought you might like to read this. Sad but honest.
    Kit

"Sad but honest"—does he mean himself or the book? I didn't think about Kit much in Miami, but now that I'm back, I get this overwhelming urge to see him, despite Seth's e-mail. And the book has given me a good excuse.

"Mee-mee." Alex toddles out of the kitchen, his arms outstretched. "Mee-mee, bickie."

"And I thought you were just pleased to see me, little man." I lift him up and swing him in the air. "Let's get you a bickie, then." Tucking him under my arm, I walk back inside and hand him a chocolate biscuit from Mum's secret stash.

"Have you got Alex?" Mum calls from upstairs.

"Yep, I'll send him up to you in a minute." (I'd better wipe away the telltale chocolate smears first.)

I clean him up with a baby wipe and then pat him on his padded-nappy bottom and carry him upstairs. He sits on the top step, staring up at me.

"See you later, alligator," I say, and gently kiss the top of his head; then I skip down the stairs and walk quickly toward the boathouse.

It's cloudy, but at least it's not raining. As I approach the boathouse, I see two figures sitting on the rocks. They are facing the window framing Kit's mobile. It's Gramps and Esther. And they're lost in conversation. I try to creep past them, but my foot crunches on some pebbles and they look up.

"Amy!" Esther smiles at me. "How was Miami?"

Gramps pats a flat stone. "I've saved you a seat."

"Miami was great," I say, sitting down. I tell them all about my holiday — although, I leave out the Matt/Sean discovery. Esther must know him, and I figure it's not my story to tell.

"Your gardener friend was looking for you," Gramps says when I've finished. "Said he had something for you."

"Yes, a book."

Esther looks at me, opens her mouth, and then closes it again. Suddenly, the sun breaks through the clouds, its rays beaming through the mobile, making the glass shards sparkle. "There you go," Esther tells Gramps, nodding at the mobile. "Told you it would happen if we waited long enough. Haven's very own northern lights, courtesy of Kit."

"Kit?" I ask her. "I thought his mum made the glass mobile."

"May? No, child. She used to collect glass paperweights, all right. Kept them in the boathouse — it was her special place — but Kit created the mobile."

"Why did he tell me his mum made it?"

Esther shrugs. "No idea. But it's the first time he's

spoken about May to anyone since the day she took her own life."

I stare at her, confused. "But I thought she died in a boating accident."

"Ach, now, I've said too much already."

"Please tell me, Esther. Please," I beg. "I'd like to know the truth."

She's silent for a moment, her eyes glassy as she stares out at the water. Finally, she says, "May rowed to the middle of the lough and lowered herself over the side. She'd filled her coat pockets with her heaviest paperweights. The weight of them sent her to the bottom. They didn't find her body for days."

My eyes fill with tears. It's so awful. Poor Kit.

She pauses and looks at me. "I know, child. Terrible, terrible thing, but the poor soul was at her wits' end. She just couldn't go on. Kit went catatonic from the shock of it. He disappeared for days. Eventually his dad found him in the boathouse. Kit had smashed the front window by hurling the rest of May's paperweights through it. They shattered on the beach. Sometimes you can still find shards among the pebbles. Afterward, Kit's dad fixed up the window, and Kit started to hang bits of the broken paperweights in it. That's how he started the mobile."

"It's so sad," I say. "But maybe there's something I can do. Maybe I could —"

"Amy." Gramps reaches out and holds my hand firmly in his. "You can't always fix people. Sometimes they're too damaged to sticky-tape back together."

"But it doesn't mean you shouldn't try," I say, jutting out my chin stubbornly.

"Aye," Esther murmurs. "That's true."

"Hey, Amy." Mum appears behind us. "Where's Alex?"

"I left him inside with you. At the top of the stairs. Ages ago."

Mum's face goes white. "I thought he was with you. He's not in the house."

I climb to my feet. "He's probably just in the garden somewhere. I'll help you look."

Mum's biting her bottom lip so hard it's gone as pale as her face.

"I'll look too," Gramps says.

"Let's all go." Esther stands up. "He can't have gone far."

Mum puts a hand up to her mouth. I can see she's starting to panic.

"Don't worry," I say. "I'm sure he's fine. He's always wandering off."

"But this is an island," Mum says. "All that water. And you know what he's like with water, Amy."

Now I'm starting to worry too. "I'll go on ahead," I say. "Gramps, you and Esther check out the garden. Mum, where's Dave?"

"On the beach with Evie and the Sticklebacks."

"You go down and get him. I'll meet you back at the house in a few minutes."

I pelt back to the house and dash upstairs to check all the bedrooms.

"What are you doing?" Denis says as I swing open the door to his room.

"Have you seen Alex?" I ask him frantically.

"He was outside playing with a dog a few minutes ago. The dog was barking a lot — I think Alex must've pulled its tail."

"The gardener's dog? The black-and-white one?"

"Yeah. Why? What's wrong?"

"Alex is missing."

"Maybe he followed the dog somewhere," Denis suggests.

"I bet you're right."

I fly out the door and down the stairs, taking them three at a time and almost twisting my ankle at the bottom. To my surprise, Denis is right behind me.

The two of us race out through the kitchen doors and almost collide with Kit.

"Seen Jack?" he asks. "I heard him barking a few minutes ago, but now he's disappeared."

"We think my little brother, Alex, is with him," I say, my heart pounding.

Kit looks at me. "I've been lifting new rosebushes across to the island from the mainland. If Jack's looking for me, he might be on the mainland. If Alex tried to follow him—"

"But he can't swim!" I screech.

Kit suddenly looks alarmed. "Quick, the tide's on the way in. Follow me."

"Tide?" I shout after him as he runs down the garden. "I thought this was a lake."

I break into a sprint, but Denis quickly overtakes me. "It's a saltwater lake," he says. "With tides. The only one in Ireland." He runs backward for a second, grinning at me, his cheeks flushed scarlet. "Come on, slowpoke. Keep up."

Who would have thought Denis was such a strong runner?

Kit turns right, past the boathouse—and then stops. The island and the mainland are separated by about six meters of water. The tide is coming in fast, and the large rocks that act as stepping stones between the two pieces of land are almost submerged.

Jack is standing on the scrubby grass of the mainland, pacing up and down and barking wildly.

"Jack!" Kit shouts. "What is it, boy?"

"He's barking at Alex," Denis says, pointing. "Look!"

Alex is lying stomach down on a large rock, clinging to strands of brown seaweed, halfway across the lake. I have no idea how he made it out that far, but that's the least of our worries. The tide is still coming in, and the waves are lapping his body. One big wave will sweep him into the water.

"Alex, stay there!" I shout. "Amy's coming." I start to make my way toward him.

He looks over and starts to wail, "Mee-mee! Mee-mee!"

"I'm coming, little man. Hang in there." I scramble across the first rock, my flip-flops sliding around. Denis is following behind me.

A wave splashes over Alex, soaking him. He lets go of the seaweed and slithers into the lake.

"Alex!" I scream, terrified. I hurry over the rocks toward him as quickly as I can, slipping on seaweed and splitting my knee open on some barnacles. It's throbbing and pumping blood, but I don't care. Hauling myself upright, I keep going.

By the time I reach his rock, Alex's head has disappeared under the water. I scour the surface with my eyes, willing him to come up, but he doesn't. My whole body goes icy with horror.

And then *SPLASH*, Kit dives into the lake. I watch transfixed as he ducks under the water and comes back up with Alex in his arms. Alex is coughing and spluttering, but he's alive.

Clinging to the rock with one arm and gasping for air, Kit holds Alex tightly against his chest with the other. "It's OK, I've got you," he tells him. Alex is thrashing around, goggle-eyed and clearly petrified.

I run toward them, not caring if I slip again, and miraculously I make it in one piece.

"Can . . . I . . . pass him . . . up . . . to you?" Kit says, his breath labored.

"Yes." I reach down and lift Alex out of Kit's arms, but his sodden weight makes me stumble forward. Just before I lose my balance and fall into the water, someone grabs me from behind and pulls me back.

Denis!

I sit down on the rock, Alex bundled in my arms.

"Mee-mee," he says, and smiles at me with blue-tinged lips.

I hold my baby brother tightly against my chest and cry with relief. "Thanks, Denis," I say through my tears.

"'S OK. Is Alex all right?" Denis looks worried.

"He will be — thanks to you and Kit."

Kit hauls himself out of the water and stands beside us, dripping. "That was close," he says. "Another couple of seconds . . ." He trails off.

Alex begins to shiver violently, his teeth rattling in his mouth, like a cartoon character's.

"You need to take off his wet clothes or he'll get hypothermia," Denis says. "They're always going on about it in Scouts. Here" — he whips off his rugby shirt and hands it to me — "put this on him."

I pull off Alex's soggy clothes and nappy and wrap him in Denis's shirt. He's still shivering. I'm about to take off my own T-shirt to put around him too — which would be so embarrassing in front of Kit — when there's an engine noise and a boat pops around the edge of the island. Inside it are Mum, Dave, and Prue. I've never been so happy to see anyone in my whole life.

Kit and Denis look relieved too. We all wave and shout, "Over here!"

Dave powers the boat toward us, almost crashing into the rock in his eagerness.

"Is Alex OK?" Mum asks as the boat draws alongside the rock. Her eyes are red and swollen.

"He's fine, Mum. Just a bit wet and shaken."

She closes her eyes for a second and blows out her breath. "Thank God."

Dave stands to take Alex. He throws the wet clothes into the bow, then passes Alex to Mum.

"Here, Sylvie." Prue hands Mum a blanket.

Swaddling Alex in it, Mum rocks him against her chest. "Oh, my baby," she croons, tears pouring down her cheeks. "My little baby. You're safe."

"What happened?" Dave asks me.

"Alex followed Kit's dog onto the rocks and got stuck," I explain. "He slid into the water and went under — but Kit jumped in and saved him. Then I nearly fell in, and Denis saved me. They're both heroes."

"Amy saved him too," Denis pipes up. "She pulled Alex up onto the rock."

Dave smiles at us. "You're all heroes," he says.

♥ Chapter 36

Kit and I climb back across the rocks to the island.
Dave offered us a lift in the boat, but Kit said he'd
walk, and I didn't want to leave him.

Once on dry land, Kit picks up his runners and
we make our way back towards the boathouse. Neither of us says a word until we get there.

Then Kit looks at me. "That was pretty intense."
He wipes some drips of water off his forehead.

"If it wasn't for you—" I begin.

"'S nothing," he cuts in. He starts to walk toward
the boathouse door. "See you later, I guess."

"Wait!" I don't want him to go. "It was your
first time in the water since your mum's accident,
wasn't it?"

He looks at me carefully. "You know, don't you? About Mam."

I nod. "Esther told me. I'm so sorry. It must be hard for you."

He nods once and stares down at the ground.

"Oh, and I meant to tell you," I continue. "Sean sent his regards. Said to say he was sorry to hear about your mum. He was very fond of her. Thought she was quite something."

He lifts his head. "Mam liked him too." His eyes well up and he whispers, "God, I miss her," under his breath. Then he shakes himself and turns away, clearly embarrassed. "I'd better get going, Amy," he mumbles.

I put my hand on his arm. "Kit, wait. I miss my granny too; I think about her a lot. She died a few years ago." I pause. "It's OK to miss someone — it means you loved them a lot. But Gramps says you have to get on with your life, even if you're sad sometimes."

We stare at each other silently for a few seconds. His eyes seem softer, more gentle, like a seal's. His hair is still wet from the water. Suddenly I remember I haven't thanked him for what he's just done — not properly, anyway.

"Thank you," I say, "for saving Alex like that.

You're amazing." And before I know what I'm doing, I lean forward and kiss him on the cheek. His skin feels soft and cool under my lips.

He looks at me, then nods once. "No bother." He breaks the gaze and walks away.

"Bye, then," I murmur to his back.

Clover is standing on the patio when I get back to the house. She runs toward me as soon as she spots me. "Where were you?" she asks. "I was worried about you."

"I was talking to Kit," I say. For some reason I don't want to tell her about the kiss. I want to keep it all to myself — my summer secret.

"Is he OK?" Clover asks. "Esther says it's the first time he's been in the water since his mum drowned."

"I hope he is." I shiver. My clothes are soaked through from holding Alex, and my knee is still bleeding: I'm a mess. "I'm dying for a shower. Let's go inside."

"I'm so darned proud of you, Beanie." She puts her arm around my shoulder. "My little Wonder Woman. I'll make you some hot chocolate. With cream and marshmallows."

I grin. "Thanks, Clover."

*　*　*

♥ Chapter 37

"Good-bye, Room That Taste Forgot," I whisper, running my fingers over the feathers at the base of the lamp shade for the very last time. I walk out backward, taking one final look, and then close the door firmly behind me.

It's chaos in the kitchen. Mum's clearing out the fridge, filling a rubbish bin with bits of leftover fruit and veg for the compost heap. Prue keeps pulling things out again and putting them aside. "We shouldn't be throwing away perfectly good food," she is saying. "If you won't take the carrots, I'll have them."

Mum smiles. "Three wilting carrots won't get you very far, Prue, but you're welcome to them."

Since yesterday the ice between Mum and Prue has definitely thawed. Mum says Alex's accident helped them both put things in perspective.

Dave and Dan are ferrying the bags across, from the island to the cars, and Denis and Clover are watching the babies. Since the rescue, Denis is a changed boy: helpful and even polite. I keep waiting for him to stick his tongue out at me, but it hasn't happened. And he's taking his new role as Alex's protector very seriously — he's not letting him out of his sight.

Mum sends me upstairs to do a final check of the children's bedrooms to make sure we don't leave anything behind. I haven't seen Kit since yesterday. I'm a bit embarrassed after the kiss, but I still want to say good-bye. I reach under Denis's bed to pull out a dusty sock and then check the window one final time.

And there he is — just below me on the patio. I'm about to shout down to him when I see he's on the phone.

"Ah, Da," he's saying. "I don't know. I haven't been fishing for a long time. . . . OK, I'll think about it." And then he laughs. His whole face lights up and his cheeks dimple. "A hero? Go 'way out of that. I'm just glad the lad's OK. . . . I'll see you later. . . .

Yes, yes, I promise. At home. . . . Bye." Kit stares at the phone for a second before walking toward the kitchen door.

It's only then that I notice Clover standing behind me.

"Are you all right?" she asks me quietly.

"What do you mean?"

"I know you like him. It's hard to say good-bye, isn't it?"

I nod. "He's just so different from the boys in Dublin. But I don't know him, not really. Not like I know Seth. It was only a holiday thing. A baby-size crush. His life is here. I can't see him living in a city, can you?"

"Nope. He needs space, like a wild animal. This is his kingdom." She stops. "He'll be fine, Beanie; you can't fix everyone."

"I know . . . Gramps said that too — but I can try."

She smiles. "That's why I love you. Ever the optimist. Now, go and say good-bye to Kit properly. You'll kick yourself if you don't."

She's right. I walk downstairs and out through the French doors. He's still on the patio.

He turns around at the sound of my footsteps. "I was looking for you, Amy," he says. "You're off this morning, aren't you? Here. It's for you." He takes something wrapped in midnight-blue velvet off the patio table and hands it to me carefully.

I peel back the velvet and stare at the paper-weight in my hands. It's the one I had admired in the boathouse — the selkie woman. "But I can't," I say awkwardly. "It's too much. You've already given me a book."

"Please. I want you to have it. To remind you of Haven. And to say thanks."

"For what?"

"For making me think. I've talked to Da, and I'm moving home in September. It's time. I might even go to horticultural college or something." He leans over and kisses me on the cheek. My skin tingles under his firm yet soft lips. "You're amazing too, Amy," he says. Then without another word, he walks down the lawn, Jack by his side.

I watch him until he disappears. "Bye," I whisper, my cheek still tingling.

Before I get the chance to recover, Dave nabs me. He seems excited, like a five-year-old who's just been given a new bike. "Amy, I need your help." He tells me what he's hoping to do. "Do you think it will work?"

"Are you sure about this?" I ask.

"Yes! Positive. That business with Alex really cleared my head."

"In that case, of course I'll help you. I have an idea. . . . "

Chapter 38

On the way back to Dublin, we're all meeting at Inchydoney Beach for one last shared lunch in a swish hotel. It's Dan's treat; he's in on the plan—but Prue's not. Dan's not all that sure she'll approve.

Once the cars are packed up, Clover and I dash on ahead in her Mini. We take Denis along for the ride.

"Right, Denis, you're on the first word," I say as we speed off. "Clover, you're drawing the heart, and I'm writing the rest. Have we all got our sticks?"

"Yes!" Denis says enthusiastically. This morning he found us three long sticks in the garden and carved the ends into points; they make ideal quills.

"There it is." I point at the big sandy beach that has just come into view.

As Clover parks the car, I text Dave and Dan:
ARRIVED SAFELY AT BEACH. WILL TEXT WHEN DONE. AMY

"Right, troops," Clover says, climbing out of the car. "Battle stations!"

"Aye, aye, captain," Denis says.

Once we've finished writing our sand message, we guard it like Beefeaters minding the Crown Jewels. Denis frightens away two dogs who are running toward the area by waving his stick at them.

Their owner isn't amused — until he sees what we're up to. "Who's Sylvie?" he asks.

"My mum."

He looks at me a little oddly.

Then my mobile beeps. It's a message from Dave: DAN'S GOT THE KIDS. BE THERE IN A MO'. LOOK OUT FOR SYLVIE. SHE'S IN THE OTHER CAR PARK AND ON HER WAY DOWN.

"They're coming!" I yell to Clover and Denis. "Thunderbirds are go!"

As planned, Denis runs up the main steps to stall Mum. His job is to distract her to give Dave enough time to run into position on the beach, down a different flight of steps.

There's quite a crowd gathering at the top of the cliff; everyone's staring down at our heart. It's hard

271 ♥

to make anyone out, but then I spot Dave running toward us.

"Nice work," he says, puffing a little. "But the first word's—"

"No time for chatting," Clover snaps. "Stand on the X. Quick."

We run off, leaving Dave standing just inside the bottom of Clover's large sand heart.

"There's Sylvie!" Clover points at the steps.

Mum is staring down in disbelief. Then she whips around and starts walking back up the steps, away from the beach.

"Mum!" I shout, sprinting up the steps, followed by Clover.

Dave is still standing in the heart, looking forlorn. "Stay there!" I yell at him over my shoulder. "Don't move."

"Mum," I puff. (It's no joke leaping up dozens of concrete steps.) "What . . . are . . . you . . . doing?"

Mum stares at her feet and shrugs.

"Sylvie, what's the matter?" says Clover.

"Does Dave think that's funny?" Mum asks glumly.

Funny? Adults are so weird.

"Sylvie," Clover says, "you do want to marry Dave, don't you?"

"He's serious?" Mum says, her face brightening. "This isn't some sort of joke?"

"Of course he's serious, Mum," I say. "He'd hardly be standing in a wonky heart in the middle of a crowded beach otherwise, would he? He's trying to be romantic."

"Wonky?" Clover scoffs. "That heart's perfect, I'll have you know."

"But look what it says." Mum points down at the sand. Inside the heart and just to the right of where Dave is standing, it reads: MARE ME, SYLVIE.

I laugh; I can't help it. Poor Mum. "We should have checked if Denis could actually spell first. I'm so sorry. But it's supposed to say 'Marry me.' Honestly."

"Oh." Mum looks down at Dave, who's shifting from foot to foot, looking mortified.

"Sylvie, you're disappointing your bridesmaids." Clover puts her arm around my shoulders and pulls me toward her, a sappy grin on her face.

Mum looks at Clover and breaks into a smile. "In that case . . ."

Mum's eyes start to well up, and she walks down the steps toward the wonky heart. Dave beams up at her and blows her a kiss.

Bridesmaid? For my own mother! Clover has got to be kidding.

"Not so fast," I say. "I'm not wearing a pink frilly dress for anyone, even my female parental."

"Lighten up, Beanie. I'm thinking funky pink bridesmaid dresses with green sashes, pink champagne, the Golden Lions, pink tea roses or maybe peonies — Sylvie loves peonies. The registry list will be at Brown Thomas department store. Apparently, you can bring any unwanted gifts back and swap them for shoes — imagine! I'm also thinking . . ."

Oops, presents. That reminds me, I forgot to get something for Seth in Miami. What will I get him now? Then it comes to me. A copy of *Into the Wild*. I started reading it last night, and I couldn't put it down; I know Seth will love it too. I won't give him the copy Kit gave me, of course; that would be too weird. And besides, inside the front cover Kit has drawn a little selkie and written: TO AMY — A RARE TREASURE. I'll write something on the flyleaf for Seth too. Something special.

"Are you listening, Amy?" Clover says. "I'm telling you my plans for the wedding."

"*Your* plans?"

"Sorry, I'll include you in all the decision making, of course."

"I meant, what about Mum?"

Clover smiles gently. "Sylvie wouldn't have a clue. Given half a chance, she'd get married in a barn, with a barbecue and line dancing. No, if we want a stylish wedding, this has got to be our baby, Beanie. Yours and mine. Clover and Amy, wedding planners *extraordinaire*."

Uh-oh. I get the feeling Clover's about to get me into a whole heap of trouble. Again!

"Pay attention, Beanie," she says, waving her hands in the air dramatically. "I see tea lights . . . little iced fairy cakes with everyone's name on them, instead of place cards. And for the wedding cake, I'm thinking something theatrical. . . ."

 # Epilogue

NEWS FLASH ON *MOVIE EMPORIUM*'S WEBSITE

Movie star Matt Munroe has been spotted in Cork, Ireland, canoodling with a raven-haired local beauty. Her identity remains a mystery.

Matt's been in Ireland ever since his shocking announcement on *Oprah* last week that he's no teen and is actually Irish and not American at all. His tearful plea for understanding touched so many viewers that the casting agent of *Life Swap* has given him a new role as an Irish cousin.

"You know what they say," Matt's agent, Gabe Grossman, said. "All publicity is good publicity. Matt's gonna be the new twenty-something heartthrob. Watch out, Zane Danvers!"

And, in a shock move, Matt granted his first post-*Oprah* interview to Irish teenzine the *Goss*. "After all, I am Irish," he said.

Acknowledgments

Heaps of thanks to . . . first and most important, my own family: my partner, Ben; my very helpful son, Sam, chief Facebook and music adviser; and my littlies, Amy and Jago, for keeping out of my study when I'm trying to write (most of the time!). Jago, I have almost forgiven you for sitting on my keyboard and making the *M* stick. Almost!

My best friends, Nicky and Tanya, who after years and years of tolerating my weird writerly moods are still talking to me, which is always a bonus. My friend Andrew, who tries to help me understand the strange world of boys. My writing friends, especially the lovely Martina Devlin, for the lovely long walks that stop me going completely bonkers. And my fellow "tween and teen" writing friend Judi Curtin, who is always such a tonic to talk to.

The gang at *wunderbar* Walker Books have been cheerleaders for Amy Green from the very start, for which I'm *très, très* grateful. Many air kisses to my clever editor, Gill Evans, who put Band-Aids on this book when it needed it; the lovely Jo Hump-D and her equally lovely Puggy, for tea parties and all kinds of fab pink things; the super-fab Annalie Grainger, who polished *Summer Secrets* until it gleamed; Alice "Blooming Brilliant" Burden, for always being fun to hang out with; and Katie Everson, for the beautiful cover. And last but most certainly not least, the man who squeezed a copy of *Boy Trouble* into every available nook and cranny in Ireland, the one, the only . . . come on down, Mr. Conor Hackett! Plus the rest of the wizard Walker sales and marketing teams. You rock, ladies and gents.

To my Team U.S.A. at Candlewick Press: Karen Lotz, Sarah Ketchersid, and Liz Zembruski for all their support and work on the Ask Amy Green tales, and for the glowing covers. The *Summer Secrets* jacket is such a joyful, soul-soothing color and I adore those flip-flops!

Kate Gordon is my special teen adviser, and a big shout-out to all her class, third-year in Rathdown, Glenageary, County Dublin. Hi, girls! I'll be back to visit you soon — promise!

And huge thanks to the Starbucks girls: Kate, again (did someone mention child labor? I hope not — I pay her in books, promise!), Isabel, Emma, and Sinéad, my crack teen research team, for divulging all their secrets.

Children's booksellers rock the planet. And a big thanks to my buddies in the biz — most especially the amazing David O'Callaghan, for the inspiration and support. Seth isn't in this one much, Dave, but he of the guyliner will be back, cross my heart — thanks for making *Boy Trouble* book of the month and for the fabby diaries!

Special thanks to Bob and all in Hughes for also making *Boy Trouble* book of the month. Color me chuffed. And the gang in Dubray, who are always so welcoming.

Mags, Tom, and Jenny in Children's Books Ireland are fantastic and their work with books and authors is the stuff of legend. Keep it up, folks!

To the good people at Annaghmakerrig, a most scenic writers' retreat — thanks for all the peace and quiet, and the food. *Summer Secrets* is a better book because of it.

And finally to the hundreds of readers who have sent me letters, e-mails, short stories, photos, and drawings—I salute you! You make writing worthwhile. Thanks so much for taking the time to contact me. I heart you all! I love to hear from you, so please do write (sarah@askamygreen.com). I'll get back to every one of you eventually—I promise. And as my daughter, Amy, always says, a promise is a promise.

All the best,

Sarah XXX

www.askamygreen.com

Meet Amy and her super-cool aunt Clover as they
take on the advice column of teen mag *The Goss*,
in the first book in the Ask Amy Green series.

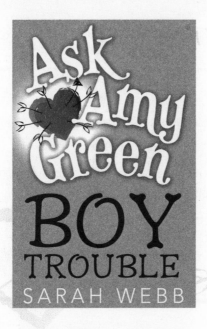

Ask Amy Green
Boy Trouble

SARAH WEBB

www.candlewick.com

Find Amy Green online at

 www. ASKAMYGREEN.COM

* Find out more about the books
and about Sarah Webb

* Get expert advice on everything from
fashion to hair care to boys — of course!

* Follow Amy Green's daily life on her blog

* And much, much more!